HEADLESS VICTORY

Other books by DAVID S. LIFSON:

The Yiddish Theatre in America
Epic and Folk Plays of the Yiddish Theatre

Contents

1 *Dramatis Personae* — 1
2 *Mise-en-Scène* — 10
3 Show Biz — 20
4 Passions Spin the Plot — 32
5 From the Top — 39
6 The Blocking — 48
7 Between the Lines — 54
8 Secondary Plot — 61
9 Private Lives — 69
10 Ingenue and Juvenile — 79
11 Places, Please! — 87
12 The Actors Prepare — 95
13 The Director's Dilemma — 104
14 Break a Leg — 116
15 Confrontation — 125
16 Curtain Going Up — 131
17 An Unexpected Ad Lib — 139
18 An Actor's Role — 148
19 Denouement — 158
20 Mummers and Men — 166

HEADLESS VICTORY

1

Dramatis Personae

There would come a time on opening night, when the curtain had descended on the second act and during the intermission of the world premiere of *Forever Yours*, that Vergil Davis would gleefully tell Marc Denis, "Two down and one to go. We're in—but big!" But the last act was to have a shattering climax that was not in the script. The crushing tragedy shocked the entire troupe and the audience out of their opening night euphoria.

The murder was the lead item on the eleven o'clock news on the airwaves that night, and the drooling readers of the next morning's headlines reveled in the juicy details of the bizarre lives of their film and stage stars. It assured colorful gossip for the ensuing Fourth of July weekend.

The murder devastated an already demoralized Marc, not only because it aborted his hopes for a new life with its glorious promise, but also because he blamed himself for his failure to act in time to forestall the frightful crime. When he first received the ominous threats, he should have rushed to the police. How futile and frivolous were his fears and rationale that by so doing his own past would have been revealed and the summer's gambit thereby destroyed. Now, in the wake of this deadly horror, an investigation that surely must follow would inevitably disclose his true identity.

No matter how much Marc tried to absolve himself from

blame, he knew that his forebodings following each portentous event during the past two weeks inexorably led to this "moment of truth." The warnings of the hovering, impending doom had clamored for attention and action. But, as the director, his professional obsession forced him to sneer at his fears and suspicions, and to dimiss from his total preoccupation and consideration anything but the play.

He allowed himself a rueful sigh when he recalled the highly abundant promise of success at the start of the season. Amidst the turmoil around him, Marc isolated himself in time and compulsively immersed his recollections into those intense and frenetic days from the first day of rehearsal of this ill-omened production.

Marc Denis had been reading to the assembled cast for almost two hours, yet his uninhibited gestures, his clear, crisp voice, his animated enthusiasm were as fresh as when he had started the play. Only he knew that his facile characterizations, his seemingly total involvement with the reading, were but a glib façade that covered his terror. Usually, at the first reading of his plays, he was always nervously apprehensive about its reception by the professionals of the theater.

He had been more than customarily nervous that morning before he came to the Town Hall Theatre, for this was his first opportunity after an involuntary ten years' hiatus. He was not fearful of what might happen to him physically—that did not even enter his mind, even though the letter implied possible violence to him. He was no coward, at least not morally, as he had amply demonstrated during the witch hunt. He could easily have succumbed to the pressures during those dismal, dark, anguished ten years by getting off the blacklist simply by making the required statements to the Congressional Committee and to the legal department of his studio. And now when he looked forward to his triumph, to a vindication, to some meaning for his ordeal, to a reward for what had been denied him and for what he had endured—was it all to be wiped out? The Kafkan threat that had hovered over him had not been as direct in all its fearfulness as this new, shocking development. On his way to the Town Hall that morning, he had picked up his mail at the village post office. First he had read with eagerness the gratifying letter from his son, who ardently described his introduction to the Skowhegan Art School where he was to spend this summer. Then, after perfunctorily glancing through some bills, he thrust them into his pocket. The odd looking letter that had his name and address typed in hand script had a suggestion of personal intimacy. Its contents stunned him.

"Knock it off, buddy. You got away with plenty so far, but your time is up. Your play won't open! Be wise and leave now. If you don't, someone is going to get hurt—bad! If you're the bleeding heart you pretend to be, you won't even start rehearsals."

A practical joke? Some prank of a demented mind? But aren't demented minds dangerous?

He had walked falteringly toward the theater. The peaceful, bucolic commons across the road from the Town Hall appeared innocent, and a haven from the horrible uncertainties that had tormented him. The giant oaks provided blessed shade from the intense mid-morning sun for the white houses with their almost black trim, and offered that never-never peace he desperately needed. He had seen the white-and-blue prowl car of a state trooper slowly drive past. Yes, he would take the letter to the police.

As he approached the stage door, he had almost resolved to take the letter to the police. His thoughts were arrested by an odd-looking, tow-headed character, almost an albino, who accosted him at the entrance. Marc waved him away as he rushed into the building, torn by fear and his native queasiness that compelled him to flee from anything unpleasant. But why fear this stranger? Had he become paranoid? Well, he thought, paranoia would be natural after receiving such a letter!

Ah, blessed, blessed purposefulness! Thus he had resolutely plunged into the first reading of the play to the cast. Throughout the reading, however, no matter how intensely concentrated his attention appeared to be focused on the play, he suspiciously peered into the dark auditorium and then out through the stage door into the sunlit field beyond. He thought he saw a figure lurking in the auditorium, but he was not sure. He definitely did see the state trooper's prowl car pass by beyond the field.

The assembled actors were enraptured as Marc came to the final scene and the end of the reading.

"We come to the final scene, an epilogue to the courtroom scene and to the play. Everett and Valerie have been brought into the judge's chamber after Everett's sentence for the attempted murder of Sinclair Turner has been suspended. The two are alone. There is an awkard silence.

Valerie finally speaks:
Valerie: What now?
Everett: I'm not allowed to leave the state for a year.
Valerie: Shall I stay?
Everett: It's pointless. You're free. The sooner you establish residence in Reno or Mexico and get the divorce the better.
Valerie: It needn't be that way.
Everett: It's no use discussing it. I can't blame you. You're human ... (with a sheepish laugh), aren't we all ...
Valerie: If you would only believe the truth ... if you would only try ...
Everett: I don't want to discuss it, ever and forever. It's all over.
Valerie: You'll be all alone. What will you do? Let me help ...
Everett: Never ...
Valerie: Never ... So final ... so ... so much like forever. (She walks toward the door, then turns and impetu-

Dramatis Personae

ously embraces him.) Ah, Scotty, not forever. Remember, I'm yours forever.
    Everett: *(He stands motionless while she leaves. Then he speaks.)* Forever, forever yours, all my love, all my life go with you forever...."

Marc paused, turned the final page, and looked up. "And so the curtain falls on the end of the play."

He pushed his chair back from the table and gratefully acknowledged, despite his inner turmoil in preoccupation with the letter, the spontaneous and sustained applause of the group. A gnawing cynicism within him appraised the applause, welcome as it was, by recalling that such excited applause was inevitable, practically a knee-jerk reflex by all actors after the reading of a play in which they would appear. None, to his recollection, had ever discussed with the author or director the play's literary values, nor anything but their individual roles. Perhaps that was as it should be, because the actors usually performed well. Nonetheless, he was interested in their reactions to the play.

Sam Dobrow was the stage manager. Since receiving his bachelor's degree, he had telescoped six years of concentrated experience as stage manager in various summer-stock companies, and now, at age twenty-seven, he considered himself a veteran. He covered his furtive glances toward the three principals with loud cheers of "bravo." The trio, sitting separately and apart from each other, politely clapped their hands, while their faces betrayed no emotion, no response to the reading of the play—a play that laid bare the intimate drama of their own lives. Sam turned to see how the reading had affected an outsider, Ellen Everhope. She was walking toward Marc with unabashed, infectious excitement. Sam was content that he had succeeded in urging Vergil Davis to engage her as the ingenue for the summer. Yes, no matter how chaotic and maddening this preliminary week for the summer-stock season, the prospect of being close to her all summer chased all problems and worries from his mind. Ellen clutched her script to her bosom while she animatedly told Marc how much she loved the play.

Everett Scott rose and approached Marc. His voice had an obviously contrived casualness.

"To keep the record straight, those were not my final words at that time."

The others all looked at him in silence. Uh uh, thought Sam. Here it comes, the first crisis of the season. It inevitably happens in the close, intense relationships of a troupe when all its members are thrown tightly together, day and night, rehearsing all day, performing together each night, sharing dressing rooms and toilets, and none with cars to flee for a few hours' respite from the grueling demands of the theater. But now? The first day? For Sam, Everett Scott had a quiet dignity that was in keeping with his handsome, resolute face and bearing, still youthful despite the graying temples. Sam figured him to be in his mid-forties. He would have typecast Scotty as Professor Higgins in *Pygmalion* but not as a droll character in a Noel Coward play, for as much as he struck Sam as being a helluva nice guy, he didn't seem to have any sense of humor, Sam decided. His former wife, Valerie Walker, appeared too young and provocatively beautiful to be the mature leading lady for the company, yet, she, too, must be in her early forties. Sinclair Turner sarcastically interrupted Sam's speculations.

"Why not tell us what they really were? We may not be able to improve our lives at this stage of the game, but we may be able to improve the script with your deathless dialogue ..."

Deliberately and patiently, Marc quickly waved aside his own annoyance at the sarcasm and Everett's anticipated retort, for Everett had suddenly flushed and whirled around toward Sinclair. The latter's feigned look of innocence but weakly covered what Everett construed to be a sneer. Marc was businesslike and unemotional as he explained.

"The author has been faithful to the facts as he knows them

Dramatis Personae 7

and in his respect for the integrity of the characters. The situation was colorful and dramatic enough in its own way without his having to make any effort to embellish it. I could go into a lengthy explanation about the art of dramaturgy and at what point reality must yield to theater conventions and dramatic urgencies. But this is summer stock and we've no time for a course in play-writing. Only because this is a new play have I consented to a reading before we plunge into rehearsals. Now, a few important points before we break for lunch. I want you to know what I expect from each of you as an individual and collectively as an ensemble. This afternoon we block act 1. Tomorrow morning we block acts 2 and 3. Tomorrow after lunch we start rehearsals from the top. The bulletin board downstairs will advise you of any changes in the schedules. I'm free evenings, this week only, so I can work individually with you should you ask me. But we must abide by Equity rules about no extra rehearsal hours. Any questions?"

A strange voice from among the dark seats at the back of the auditorium gasped out as if its owner was struggling for air after a deep plunge into a pool.

"Yes. W-w-why is the focus mostly on the attempted murder and psychiatry? Why not on poetry and love?"

While the others remained silent and turned toward the voice, Marc rose and walked to the edge of the stage to peer into the darkness. A figure had risen and walked down the aisle toward him. When it emerged from the dark, Marc saw the tow-headed, albinolike youth whom he had avoided earlier that morning. The youth kept talking with a mouth full of saliva, which made his remarks almost unintelligible. Both the intrusion and the giggles he heard from the group on stage behind him irritated Marc so that he found himself snapping at the interloper.

"Visitors are not allowed at rehearsals."

"I'm sorry . . . b-b-but I've been waiting outside to see you . . ."

"Well, wait outside then." The tow-head disappeared up the aisle and out the front door. Marc returned to his seat and repeated, "Any questions?" He looked around. There were no questions. He would have liked to ask them a few questions about that damned letter. The reading and his assertion of authority had purged him of the whining paranoia with which he had first reacted to the letter. He had really anticipated no questions from the troupe, so confident was he of his craftsmanship. And, after all, they were all seasoned troupers. Even Ellen had had two seasons in summer stock and knew the routine. As for Joseph Jr., he had been brought up in the world of the theater. His own questions would wait for the appropriate time during rehearsals. Thank heavens that brash brat of an apprentice, for once, kept her mouth shut.

Marc wasn't through—he had more to say. Sam liked that in Marc, for too many directors had such a damned superior attitude toward actors. Marc always shared his thoughts with the actors so that all of them had a concept of the whole, of what the entire play was about, rather than merely what their solitary roles were, depicted in the script sides from which they usually worked, especially when the play was a recently popular Broadway success. Marc wanted them to be involved with more than their sides, which gave them no more than their cues and their own speeches. That's why Marc had arranged for all of them to have complete scripts of the play.

Marc, as a director, had an unobtrusive way of commanding attention, of getting respect. Some directors were flamboyant exhibitionists; they always interrupted rehearsals, jumped onto the stage, and pushed the actor aside with an aggressive, "Here, let me show you how to play the scene." They were more frustrated actors than directors. Marc's style, however, was one wherein he quietly took the actor aside and discussed and probed the role, always with questions to the actor as to why he did or did not do thus and so. In this fashion Marc was able to have the actor develop his attitudes, actions, and delivery of lines from the character's inner psychology, with

Dramatis Personae

valid motivations rather than the surface grafting on of an interpretation obtained through imitation of the other type of director's exhibitionism.

Sam had known Marc before he had gone to Hollywood and carved a niche for himself as a talented director. Sam had planned to follow him there, but Marc had suddenly dropped out of sight. Sam never knew why; there seemed to be some mystery attached to it. But there was no mystery about Marc's great abilities as a director, which Sam recalled from his own undergraduate days when Marc was his drama professor. But why, if Marc had dropped out of directing in films, hadn't he gone back to the stage or to a professorship? Well, maybe during the summer Sam would have a bull session with him and find out.

2

Mise-en-Scène

Marc paced about the stage and enthusiastically addressed the troupe.

"We're starting the season with an exciting play. I believe in it. I have faith in it. It's about real, honest-to-goodness people. The story line is simple, familiar as a newspaper story. It is actually the real life drama of three members of our company. Did the author go arty or take liberties with the real story in order to push for a way-out effect or for some spurious theatrical formula? No. There are no cliché situations like a glamorous star trying to stage a comeback. Through flashbacks and stream-of-consciousness flowing scenes, the author has tried to dramatize the heroic effort of Valerie Walker to stage a comeback, but a comeback as a decent human being. You will find some of the psychiatric tenets of adjustment being touched upon. But there is no men-in-white clinical bunkum; we have the confrontation of human beings in their relationships with each other in the elusive, transient world of the theater. My job as director is 95 percent done; I've got the most perfect cast . . ."

He was interrupted by cheers and a few "hear, hear!"

"Of the remaining 5 percent, 1 percent is my being traffic cop, 1 percent timekeeper, 1 percent Simon Legree to goose you along, 1 percent to worry for you, and 1 percent of the gross according to my contract."

Mise en Scène

The laughter was tentative, for most of them wondered what kind of a deal Marc had made with such a notorious chiseler like Vergil Davis. Marc continued.

"If there is a theme to the play, I offer you the one in which I believe, and it is a challenge to each of you: actors are people."

Ellen interrupted him, "Who is the author?"

"A Hollywood writer who must remain anonymous until we open in New York. O.K. now, thirty-minute lunch break."

Sam repeated the call and added, "We start at the top."

On his way out Marc stopped to instruct Sam and to make certain that the stage would be set for the first act. Sam flared up, "With whom? Where in hell are all the apprentices Davis promised us? And who's going to play the judge? Maybe Davis himself—ugh!"

Marc grinned at him. "Patience, Sammy boy, this is only the beginning of the season. Save your steam for the big crises."

If only Marc weren't so paternalistic, thought Sam. How philosophic can he get! Sam pictured himself in a car hurtling toward a head-on collision, and Marc, alongside him, calmly reflecting on the relative velocity of the two cars and the force of the impact. Sam assured Marc that he could take it; he'd been around. "But my trouble is that I believe people—a promise is a promise. Davis promised me fifteen apprentices, and all we've got is that infant with her Freudian fixation, and all those psychiatric clichés that I'm ready to scream. And where is that scenic designer? He was due here at nine, and it's noon now."

Marc thought for a moment, then suggested that Sam get Joseph Jr. to help him. Joseph Jr.! Wow! And who was going to help him? Marc and Davis had passed the word around that this son of the famous Hollywood star, the legendary bad man of the flicks, was to be treated no differently from anyone else. Sam suspected that Joseph G. senior had kicked in some money to Davis in order to get him to hire Jr. for the company. Joseph had come late to the reading, had a punchy, glazed look, and seemed comatose all morning.

When Sam Dobrow voiced his skepticism about Joseph Jr., Marc impulsively wanted to have a private talk with the young man. He looked toward him and saw him in close conversation with Sinclair Turner. Joseph Jr. was tall and slim, with a sensitively handsome face. The older actor placed his arm around the young man's shoulder; the arm was quickly and impatiently shrugged off. Sinclair saw Marc looking at them and flushed; Marc quickly turned away. He certainly wanted no contact with Sinclair Turner other than what he was professionally obliged to accept; Sinclair would be gone after the two weeks for which he had been jobbed for this play. And if it reached Broadway, there'd be practically no reason for them to come into contact with one another.

Yet, Marc was uneasy. His momentary suspicion that Sinclair was the perpetrator of the letter was eclipsed by his sensing something unwholesome between the older man and the company's juvenile. Sinclair had a reputation as a lady's man and had probably given Scotty sufficient cause to attempt murder. But boys!? Oh well, maybe he was bisexual. If it was anything like that, Marc shrank from a confrontation. Anyhow, in two weeks Sinclair would be gone. Alas, the boy could easily be corrupted in less time. You're no goddamned psychiatrist, Marc sneered at himself, so lay off—you've got a show to put on, so get with it! He called to Joseph to help the stage manager set up.

"Can I get something to eat first, Sir? I didn't have breakfast."

Marc agreed but cautioned him to hurry back. The young man left after a grateful "thank you, Sir." Sinclair Turner left with him.

Sam Dobrow turned to Marc, "What's this 'Sir' routine?"

The stage manager should—was entitled to—know if he was to contend with the vagaries of the members of the company and, despite them, make certain the production ran

Mise en Scène 13

smoothly. So Marc stopped to explain.

"Military school. His mother sent him to military school so he would not be in the way when she ran a party and opened the second swimming pool for the guests, or showed off her art collection. That 'sir' business is the least of his problems."

"I'm going on record now," Sam emphatically replied. "His problems won't be my problems and not the problems of back stage."

Reassuring him, Marc offered to bring back lunch for Sam. The stage manager ordered coffee and a hamburger with plenty of onions and relish, then turned to his work while Marc disappeared up the aisle and through the door at the front of the house.

But Sam was puzzled. Military school, he mused; I thought the old man was a progressive. To be the great character actor for which he was famed required a sensitivity. He had one of the most famous art collections in Hollywood. What has that to do with it! Maybe it's just social snobbery. But during the thirties, so Sam had heard, the old boy had been connected with so many progressive causes. Maybe that, too, was a pose, for he quickly left films to go on the stage with that anti-Communist play *Light in the Night*, and many had suspected that he did it to prove to the witch hunters that he was clean. Ah, actors—what they wouldn't do for their careers!

Dismissing these thoughts, he turned to laying out the ground plan. Referring to the scene design he had unrolled on the table, and with masking tape in hand, he started to place strips of tape on the floor. He soon needed help to shift chairs that were to be placed to represent the doors and windows. He turned to the nubile apprentice who sat mooning. She became aware of his glare and jumped up to help. She wore tight-fitting cut-down jeans and a knit shirt with a deep neckline. Wow, he gulped, she isn't wearing any bra, and those pointed nipples are going to pop through. For her scant sixteen or seventeen years she was some hunk of woman! Marilyn worked well, most efficiently. If only she wouldn't keep jabbering away with her misinformed, cliché-filled Freudian interpretations of everything she heard, read, or experienced.

While they worked, she pontificated about the psychiatric misinformation in the play. If it were up to her, she would cut out the first and third acts and start all over again with a rewrite based on the second act. Of course, Everett Scott's possessiveness, popularly known as jealousy, which led to the shooting, was a clear case of anal retentiveness, and the shooting was a sublimated and symbolic homosexual gesture. Sam wasn't even listening. He tried to distract her from her unrelenting preoccupation by intermittently responding with imitations of Peter Lorre, Greta Garbo, Marlon Brando as Stanley Kowalski, and Cary Grant. The word *psychoanalysis*, which she used with unwarranted authority, annoyed him. If anyone need psychoanalysis for adjustment, he would soon be the candidate if he had to put up with the whimsicalities of the scene designer, Bobby Francis.

What in hell do they teach them up there at Yale! The confounded ground plan would suit Radio City Music Hall or some arena theater, or maybe the barn they have as a theater at Yale, but it's completely out of whack for this town-hall stage.

Sam's grumbled annoyance with the scene designer prompted Marilyn to rush to his defense. Her father had been duly impressed with the idea that she'd be working with Joseph G. Heywood, Jr., but when he learned that a Yale man was on the staff as scene designer, he was ready to offer up his virginal daughter to the undying art of the theater. Someone had given her father a copy of Sinclair Lewis's *Bethel Merriday*, and that convinced him that his daughter would come home from her summer's exposure to the muse as inviolate as she was on the day she was born. That Yalee, Bobby Francis, convinced him.

I'm old before my time, thought Sam. Here I am actually listening to this TV-style dialogue and succumbing to it.

Mise en Scène

Maybe he should be more impersonal, more businesslike with this child—it's going to be a long summer—yet, who knows? She may be next year's star on Broadway, or maybe her rich father might invest in the play that he, Sam Dobrow, will one day produce on Broadway. Oh shit, why must he always figure, promote, connive . . .?

Marc would rather have avoided a meeting with the young man who had intruded upon the rehearsal. But he knew that if he did not get it over with now he would constantly have to contrive ways of avoiding him for the remainder of the summer. He decided to be firm, quick to get it over with, and coldly polite so that no matter how obtuse the other may be he'd be sure to get the hint that he was not to become a nuisance. Marc's hope that the youth, perhaps, had not waited and would be gone was short-lived. There he stood in the lobby, squinting through the thickest lens Marc had ever seen, and speaking through a mouth, when opened, that revealed pink breaches on the pinkest of gums between a quarter of the normal number of teeth. Unpressed, shiny pants of worsted pin stripes fell to above the ankles, which were covered by soiled, once-white socks that were encased in frayed, dull brown moccasins. A tieless plaid shirt, open at a too-pink neck, was covered by a tight, grayish tweed jacket with much-too-short sleeves. Marc recalled, with a feeling of revulsion, that he had refused to take an apartment in New York because on the ground floor lived a family with a hydrocephalic son who constantly sat in a wheelchair in front of the building. Marc despised himself for his self-indulgent squeamishness. For chrissakes, have some compassion, he inwardly screamed at himself.

Yet a panic seized him. He could not dispel the queasy feeling that always overwhelmed him in an encounter with something unwholesome. He wanted to flee, yet he compulsively felt a compassion for this woebegotten youth and allowed himself to be drawn, as always, into a situation and contact he would have gladly avoided.

"I'm Lee Perkins ... I've been hoping to meet you."
"Hello, Lee."
The extended hand was damp when Marc grasped it.
"I didn't mean to be rude to you, but rehearsals in the professional theater are closed to visitors. I hope you understand ..."
"Oh, that's all right. I'm sorry I upset you. I've been wanting to meet you for the past two months—ever since I heard you would be here. You see ..."
"Why didn't you simply leave your name and phone number at the box office. Then I would ..."
"I didn't think, I suppose. And we don't have a phone. Maybe ..."
At this point Lee Perkins apologetically, fearfully, diffidently, and with embarrassment, groped for words. Marc tried to be helpful, but he wanted this awkward meeting to be finished, over with, and behind him.
"What can I do for you?"
"I write poetry."
"Yes?"
"I wrote a play—in verse."
Uh uh, here it comes, Marc feared. That's all I need now, to read a new play! In verse no less!
"I'm only the director. What I suggest to you is that you try to get an agent. That's the way it's done. Let's suppose I love your play. What can I do about it? An agent can get you to a producer. That's his business."
"I've been through that gambit. I wrote a play, hitch-hiked to New York, and brought it to the office of a famous producer. Y'know what happened?"
Marc knew all too well, but he dumbly shook his head in mystification.
"A very classy girl, y'know, when you get off the elevator there's this very sophisticated receptionist. 'May I help you,' she chirps out. 'Yes,' I say. 'I wrote a play and I think this

Mise en Scène

office would be ideal to produce it.' So what do you think she says?"

"I don't know."

" 'Who sent you?' Just like that. 'Who sent you?' So I think fast and say, 'God.' She looked at me like I was some kind of nut. She tried to humor me and started to laugh like it was some big joke. I told her that her outfit produced plays and I wrote them, so, naturally, I brought my play to that office. Either she felt sorry for me or she had this tape-recorder-type ploy all set up. So she says, 'We only accept plays for consideration from reputable literary agents.' So I ask her where I could find an agent. She told me to look in the yellow pages of the phone book. That's what I did. Guess what happens."

This was taking too much of his time. Marc urged the young man to walk with him toward the diner after nodding, "I could imagine." He hoped this weak expression of sympathy would shut off the other's garrulity and allow Marc to get along with his own problems.

"I don't think you can imagine it. It was like a broken record. I looked up literary agents in the phone book. I found a name that was familiar. I remembered it from something in *Writers Magazine*. I hurried over to the office, carrying with me my precious, great American play, introduced myself to the receptionist, and started to offer my play. Guess what she said."

Marc nodded his head as they both chorused in unison, "Who sent you?"

The youth, almost hysterically, gasped out, "So what do you think I answered? Yup—'God sent me.' Now you know why I was so anxious to meet you. Will you read my play? Will anyone in the theater ever read my play . . . ?"

The young man's voice was humble, frantic, pathetic—and challenging. It was the echo of all creativity clamoring to be heard, to be seen, at the very least to be acknowledged. Marc hesitated. He was, despite his appearance of calm, mentally galloping toward the police to seek protection, to find an explanation by professionals of that frightening letter in his pocket. Again he was undecided what to do. Again he weighed the possibilities as he had done so many times the past few hours. Was it from a crank or some nut? Buy why *him*? *Why*? He had come to rehearsal that morning with an uncommon confidence, something he had not felt these past ten years. And now this damned threat! Could it be the FBI? Judging by their sneaky interrogation of his friends, the certainty that he felt about his phone having been tapped or bugged or whatever they call it, he wouldn't put it past them to harass him with a threatening letter. If he went to the police, they would certainly get in touch with the federal authorities because the letter came through the U.S. Mail. That would surely bring in the FBI.

All these thoughts hurtled through his mind as he tried to avoid looking at the eager but sad young man. Why in hell me, raged Marc to himself. I'll tell him to give it to Vergil Davis—he's the producer.

As if he had read Marc's thoughts, Perkins quickly said, "Mr. Davis said I should try to get you to read it."

Dear, dear Vergil! Wouldn't he have loved to strangle him at that moment! He had to be honest with himself and with Perkins—he simply did not have the time. But Perkins was thrusting a thick manila envelope at him as he said, "Please?"

Marc looked at him, then quickly turned away from the piglike eyes so distorted through the thick lens, from the imploring, salivating mouth, and by some incomprehensible connection thought of his son who had talent—proven by his acceptance at Skowhegan. One day his son, like all creative artists, would be pleading for recognition, for appreciation, for acknowledgement, for—oh, what the hell! Yet he demurred. Perhaps if he caught the other in a lie, he could crawl out of it.

"When did Mr. Davis tell you this?"

"A few times during the last few weeks. When I was in the

Mise en Scène

box office using his typewriter. Mine's broken and I wanted to retype the last act. Delores, who works there, suggested I use it, and Mr. Davis said it would be O.K."

It sounded plausible. "All right. But I don't know when I'll be able to get to it. We're rehearsing all day, and at night I have to block out the next play that we start rehearsing next week..."

Perkin's joy was pathetic, for Marc had only said that he would read the play. The young man thrust the envelope into Marc's hands and fled as if he feared Marc might change his mind.

Marc opened the envelope while he walked and extracted the script. It was bound in thin cardboard of the kind that came in Marc's shirts when they were returned from the Chinese laundry, and the covers each had two holes around four inches apart through which a black shoelace was tied to hold the script together. On the front cover, in a surprisingly elegant flourish of Old English penmanship, Marc read the title: *Headless Victory, A Poetic Drama*, by Lee Perkins.

Marc groaned. In verse no less!

3

Show Biz

Marilyn was babbling away, passing judgments, gleaned from a few brief fifty-minute hour's sessions with a shrink, on all members of the company. Bobby Francis was, for her, a new category; one day she'd "poop him out." Joseph Jr. also was a new but familiar category; she'd gotten him classified, however. Before Sam could ask her about the special features that made up the new category, she was discussing Sinclair Turner. Ah, there was a man indeed! He had all the sinister, decadent excitement of a mature man. Yet she was torn. There was the director, Marc Denis. She was intrigued by his depth, his understanding, his sensitivity. She had given it a great deal of thought—yes, he was just the man to appreciate the fulsomeness, the vast capacity of a woman like her. In some cultures girls of her age had already given birth to five or six children. Of course she had discussed this with her father. He had squirmed in discomfort. He had thought she was *actually* propositioning *him*. Morally, she thought everyone was old-fashioned about incest. Yes, she conceded, there is much evidence, genetically, to thwart any ideas of experimentation on her part. Also, her father may be stuffy about being a pioneer or a guinea pig, no matter how scientifically important it may prove.

Despite her puerile chattering, she did work effectively, and for this Sam was grateful. But, for chrissakes, would he have to put up with this all summer? At least she quieted down at that moment when a state trooper came onto the stage from the wings. Sam smiled when he observed the trooper's healthy appraisal of Marilyn.

"She's only 16."

The trooper grinned back as Marilyn protested that she was closer to seventeen. Sam told her to go find Bobby Francis before she could pursue further talk with the newcomer. Then the stage manager asked the trooper what he could do for him; the response was that he was looking for Vergil Davis, the producer. When Sam introduced himself and suggested that he might help, the trooper riffled through some papers in his pouch and brought one out.

"I think I can help you, Mr. Dobrow. It's about the gun permit. Here, this is yours. It's a temporary permit for stage use only, please remember. Is Mr. Everett Scott around?"

"He'll be back within the half hour. If you have his gun permit, I can give it to him."

"You can tell him they're holding his up..."

The trooper hesitated, and Sam volunteered, "His police record, I guess."

"That's it, all right."

"If Scotty didn't have a police record, we wouldn't have a play. Didn't you know about it?"

When the trooper shook his head, Sam explained, "A couple of years ago he shot Sinclair Turner because he thought Turner was playing around with his wife. Turner recovered, and Scotty got off with a suspended sentence for attempted murder. Our play is about that case."

"I remember it now. I thought the name sounded familiar. Yes, and her name was Valerie Walker. Hey, you've got all three of them here—in the same play?"

"That's right. They're playing their real life roles in this play about the case. Say, don't you read the papers? We've been plugging this for weeks."

"Of course I read the papers. I didn't see it in the *Boston*

Record. But I don't follow theater news. Now I've got to explain to Mr. Davis and ask him to get a new application in, and do it in a hurry."

"He's up front in the box office..."

Marilyn quickly interrupted by offering to lead the trooper to Davis. Dobrow snapped at her to "git, and get Bobby Francis in a hurry." She waved to the trooper as she left. Meanwhile the trooper laughingly assured Sam he'd find his way, "After all, this is our Town Hall." Before he left to find Davis, the trooper asked Sam if he could ask Dr. Strong to wait for him inside; it was hot waiting out there in the sun. Sam assured him it would be all right. The trooper summoned the doctor from his car, introduced him to the stage manager, jumped down from the stage apron, and went up the aisle to the front of the house.

Without interrupting his work, Sam nodded a "hi" to the middle-aged and vigorous-looking man who entered. The doctor responded with a smile as he filled his pipe. He saw the stage manager having difficulty with holding down an end of the tape as he measured the stage floor, and he offered to hold down the end. Soon he was in his shirt-sleeves working methodically with the other man who, when they briefly paused, commented on the doctor's sophisticated expertise.

"Oh, the usual routine of college drama club. We've got our community theater group right here in town. I've acted, directed, stage managed... the works. Last winter I played Nat in *Ah, Wilderness*. The George M. Cohan role, you know."

Further talk between them revealed that the doctor was on vacation, had only seen an emergency patient that morning, and was free for a few weeks. He wondered if he could be of any use around the theater. Sam quickly assured him that he'd be a blessing and asked Dr. Strong to wait for Vergil Davis or Marc Denis.

Dr. Strong opened up his quiet reserve and smiled with enthusiasm. This would be his first experience with a real, professional company. Sam told him to count his blessings for having led a sheltered life. When the doctor waved aside Sam's cynicism, Sam told him that the only way to have a love for the theater is by retaining illusions about it, and the rat race of summer stock can destroy the most deep-rooted love for the stage. The doctor protested that there is nothing more grimly real than being a medical man, yet he retained his respect and love for his profession. At that point Sam thought that they should introduce themselves. Dr. Mitchell Strong and Sam Dobrow shook hands with warmth and sincerity.

Their conversation turned toward the play. Sam found himself enjoying talking with the doctor, so he went into greater detail about the genesis of the play and about its principals. He wondered if the people in the area would come to see it and also attend the theater through the rest of the season.

Mitchell Strong sucked at his pipe as he thoughtfully reflected on the question. His speech started slowly and then became almost lyrical in his enthusiam. "I love my neighbors, my good friends in the town and quite a few miles around. I've seen many of their insides, I can tell you." That with a chuckle. "Yes, they have their weaknesses, and that shows most when someone close to them is really sick and they look at me with dumb, scared faces—and that's their love for the sick ones. And I've gotten to love them all. Their day-to-day small talk doesn't arouse passionate feelings in me, or in any of them for that matter—it's the day-to-day sameness of unchanging time, of an unspoiled part of America. You'd think God picks them out to be born here because they fit into the landscape. This is Thoreau and Emerson country, you know. Down in Newburyport we have a statue to William Lloyd Garrison. Nothing really spectacular happens here, like I suppose it does in the theater world. We have no drugs, no delinquency, no mobsters. Oh yes, we have some grim and brutal confrontations, very dramatic, at our town meetings—really the only hundred-percent democracy in our country. Frankly, the most sensational meeting we had in years was this past spring when we all debated whether or not to have a theater troupe here and about the kind of element it will attract to our town. Your Mr. Davis is quite a good salesman. He convinced them ... "

"Did I hear my name mentioned?"

It was Vergil Davis approaching down the aisle toward the stage with the trooper directly behind him. As Davis jumped up on the apron of the stage, the trooper quickly joined him and introduced the doctor. Then, when the trooper said he was leaving with expectations in his voice that the doctor was coming along, he smiled knowingly when the doctor said he was staying. The trooper turned to Davis with, "You ought to grab Dr. Strong for your company. He's a great actor. Better than Rock Hudson or any of 'em."

As the trooper started to leave, Davis reminded him that there would be two tickets at the box office for him for opening night. The trooper demurred for a moment; he would be on duty till eight and may have to come in his uniform. Davis assured him that it would be all right. After the trooper's exit, Davis turned to Dr. Strong with cordial thanks for being on the patrons' list. The two men, in their different ways, seemed to be more mature, more urbane, more identified with the complexities of life than is usually found in the self-centered, limited personalities in the inquilinous abode of backstage. Yet, the doctor wondered about the producer. Was he really a famous producer?

Sam might have told him, but Sam was not one to gossip. And if he were obliged to say anything about anyone, he would have to tell the truth: Davis was famous for his longevity, for having survived. That feat alone marshalled all his ingenuity to connive, to scrounge, to play all the angles—and should he be blessed with a marginal, fleeting success, of course he attributed it to his own perseverance, hard work, brilliant sense of the theater, and managerial abilities. Any brief "hit" he produced carried him along for the next season, but his backers never got any profit from it—they'd be lucky if they got a fractional percentage of their investment in addiion to two opening-night seats and an invitation to the champagne (domestic) party after the curtain.

Meanwhile, the Davises of "show biz" will dissipate their nest egg between productions. When the producer finds a likely play, that has a small cast of characters and one simple set of scenery, his press agent will start the publicity build-up for the wonder man of Broadway. For the cognoscenti, with their Bessemer-like digestion, find this type of publicity an emetic far surpassing anything prescribed among the marvels of a providential medical science.

Devotees of the Sunday supplements across the nation succumb to the blandishments of his picture, to the platitudinous interviews with him, to the glamor he exudes because of his association with famous stars who have appeared in his extravaganzas. Columnists repeat every corny word that he belches forth and is planted by his publicist ad nauseum. He is hailed as patron of the arts, high priest of our nation's culture, and an instant expert on everything that flesh is heir to—for he appears on TV talk shows (for a fee, of course), and the college where he took a few extension courses will have him deliver the commencement address and reward him with an honorary doctorate, while he revels as a guest speaker at the otherwise dull meetings of equally dull cultural groups that proliferate through the land among otherwise frustrated provincial ladies. He is ever "on the make" with promising young actresses or glamor-seeking matrons. His glibness carries him through a succession of peccadilloes, and a worldly, suave manner covers a chicanery so that he disarms everyone to an extent that would make a Madison Avenue fag weep with envy. The irony of it all is that amidst all his dalliance, he makes each astute trick appear to be a selfless act of dedication to the "art of the theater!"

Suppose someone challenged Sam about his profile of the Davis type of producer, about whom he had been ruminating, with the counter argument that many of the "angels" who invest with him are astute businessmen who must have been very wise to have accumulated so much excess money to be ready to gamble by backing a play. Sam had met many of them, these investors, these "angels," a heterogeneous bunch. Some are would-be intelligentsia eager to rub elbows with glamour pusses in the scintillating theater world. Rarely there may be one odd soul who believes in some message he finds in the play. Some are simple suckers deluded into thinking the theater to be the path to a quick buck. One may be the father of a stagestruck daughter, or the rich lover of an actress for whom his investment buys a role.

But what is Davis doing in summer stock? Oh well, it's a cheap way to try out a new play. Maybe he believed in some of his own twaddle about an experimental theater, and summer stock is where he could indulge himself. Or maybe he had dreams of establishing a drama school for stagestruck kids who are too old for camp and too young to qualify for work at some routine job during the summer. He found many parents eagerly seeking a convenient parking lot for their kids while the parents disport themselves without encumbrances.

Sam had visited Davis at his home in a brownstone in Greenwich Village—the address gave the producer an aura of art, sophistication, and glamour. The apartment was furnished with relics salvaged from various plays, each making romantic conversation piece and providing the cue for Davis to inject into a conversation with a visitor the name of a famous actor or actress—no one could compete with him as name-dropper—who had appeared in one of Davis's productions and has, since, had a successful or bizarre career, all of which puts the visitor into a state of euphoria. His shabby walls made a gallery of enchantment with colored sketches of stage settings of his productions.

Strewn about his large studio-living room in calculated disorder were books on the theater, on art, on music, and manuscripts of unknown and helplessly hopeful playwrights—all of which he had never read—that served to establish incontrovertible proof that he is one of the few erudite men in the theater. He was usually six months past due on his rent both for his apartment and for his chi-chi office—and why not, he owed money to everyone. When he was obliged to travel to his office by subway, it hurt his sensitive, aesthetic soul—his parents came from a hovel with an outhouse in Bukovina, by steerage to America!

But Sam has seen Davis in action, with an acumen that gets things done in the fickle world of the theater. Alas, the theater needs these operators who know all the shortcuts that make the raising of the curtain possible. How different from all the parsimonious living are the days and nights when they are in production—after the angels have come across with their checks and the thousands of dollars are in the bank, and the Actors' Equity Association bond has been posted. Davis has found a play, and the metropolitan press eagerly quotes his publicity release to the world. In the furious, exhilarating, lush days of production, life becomes beautiful for him. His popularity is at its zenith, while his backers have impressive-looking legal papers that assure them of a pro rata participation, according to their investment, in fifty percent of the production—the producer retains the other fifty per cent.

What a change in his style of living now! He immediately puts himself on the new company's payroll, at anywhere from five hundred to a thousand dollars a week; he hires assistants from among his leeching, indigent relatives, each of whom will "kick back" to him part of his official salary; he pays up his back rent; he starts dining regularly at Sardi's (charging the tab to the production budget); he makes deals for payola with scene studios, costumers, printers—from each of whom he gets his cut; and if he hasn't been too deeply in debt, he will be able to stash away a few grand after paying up delinquent bills. Thus he will have a nest egg to tide him over should the Olympian critics be less than enthusiastic about his production.

Should the play succeed and then be sold to the films, ah, then the Davises may have the strength of character to invest for themselves part of it in AT&T or in a refuge out on Long Island. Oh yes, the angels will first receive, periodically, parts of their investment and, if the success is substantial, all of it and then percentages of the profits. If the play quickly folds, they lick their wounds by taking a tax loss, and the producer begins to cultivate a new crop of prospective angels for his next venture.

Yet, Sam recalled the time before he entered the profession, when he went to the theater, sat in the plush upholstered seats that became his magic carpet, when the lights dimmed and the curtain rose, and he edged forward in his seat, for then he was not merely in a theater—he was in the scene on stage, in the lives, in the very breath of each character. Transported, he did not know about the machinations of the Davises. Now he reasoned, don't the Davises make all that possible? Don't they serve the necessary function of the midwife? He thought back about the legendary figures in the theater: how about David Belasco, Arthur Hopkins, and ...? They, too, had to scrounge and connive. But then, there were the Group Theater, the Theatre Guild, and the Playwright Company. And, without a Davis to find it, promote it, assemble its parts, will the new play ever be produced? Sam rationalized that most fields of business have promoters, many more unsavory than found within the purview of the theater therefore, why not in the theater.

Sam was confident of Davis's response when he told him of Dr. Strong's interest in the theater and wish to be part of the company. Davis quickly made certain that the doctor wasn't interested in being house physician for a fee. Sam reminded him that the role of the judge was not filled and that Dr Strong might be interested in reading for it, and he added that the doctor was on vacation for a few weeks and available. The doctor eagerly suggested that he'd even be interested in just working backstage if there was no role for him. Davis asked him if he was a member of Equity, and when Strong said he wasn't Davis enthusiastically urged him to wait to see Mar

Denis—"When it comes to casting, he's the doctor, ha ha."

As Strong accepted the copy of the play the stage manager thrust upon him, he asked if he could be told a little about the play and his role so that he wouldn't be reading entirely "cold." Before Sam could respond, Davis hastened to explain.

"It's about a couple of wonderful human beings, our stars, Valerie Walker and Everett Scott. You know, this is not just another production for me. I've produced plenty. These two kids, Valerie and Scotty, I gave them their start in the theater. Yes sir, I took them on a USO tour of *Golden Boy*. They fell in love and got married. You know—clean, decent kids. I was their best man. Then, when we got back stateside, they both started to score—you know, they became real hot properties. Oh my, they were getting right to the top. Then Scotty had to get himself involved with some of these loudmouthed Reds. Producers started to worry about him, drawing too much attention to himself for the wrong reasons. Soooo, he just couldn't get a job. Valerie was all set to go on tour with a revival of *The Glass Menagerie* when the scandal broke. Basically, the facts are in the script. You know something, I feel like a father to them. I hope this play, this chance for them to get together again, will straighten them out. Yes sireee, the play's the thing."

Davis took an extra script from the stage manager and handed it to the doctor with the suggestion that he look through it, with careful note of the judge's role, and be ready to read for Marc Denis. Sam told him to look through the second scene of the first act and the third scene of the last act. The doctor took the play and excused himself with the observation that he could best concentrate outside among the trees behind the stage entrance to the town hall.

Following the doctor's exit, Sam turned upon Vergil Davis with the accusation that he was promised many apprentices to help him. All he had was the loquacious Marilyn to help him hold book at rehearsals, while he had to be nursemaid to the cast, to be timekeeper and coordinator for the scene designer, to keep the technician with his lighting effects on cue, to be responsible for costumes, furniture, props, and stage dressing—meanwhile "that Yalee scene designer was three hours late!"

The producer grinned at him with "That's summer stock, a crisis every hour on the hour." Then he challenged Sam with the observation that he had been in summer stock and knew the score before he undertook this job as stage manager. He covered the challenge with, "and I knew what I was doing when I hired you. You're no baby, you know your business and I'm confident you and your director will give us a damned good, professional show." Meanwhile, he told Sam, his publicity was a week late, the local Boy Scouts and Girl Scouts had not yet consented to be the ushers, program advertisers had not paid their bills—and the local newspapers were pressing for payment for the ads, Equity wanted an additional bond, and his car had broken an axle "on these damned bumpy, country back roads."

The producer's breezy exit left a disgruntled and frustrated Sam to cope with the urgencies of the production. Although the physical and practical obstacles that confronted him challenged his professionalism, occupied his immediate thoughts and his customary pragmatic attitudes and approach to problems, he was bedeviled by an uneasy foreboding. Yes, Marc had sailed through the productive morning with a surface confidence. But why had Marc become so jumpy when the voice from the dark auditorium interrupted them? Why had Marc seemed to be, in face of the demands of the reading of the play, immersed in thoughts that had nothing to do with the moment? To Sam, who knew Marc so well, it was very unlike the director to be so preoccupied by an ominous something apart from the production of *Forever Yours.*

Sam sang under his breath, "The show must go on," and sighed as he thought that he should abide by his grandfather's advice, "Don't get involved—don't stick your neck out." Only for a fleeting moment he thought of the rewards from a successful production, the loot for the producer, the money and fame for the author, ditto for the stars and director; but the stage manager who was den mother to the cast, who was the nursemaid for all associated with the production for which he had been the pivot and fulcrum that kept it on course, who was... oh well, it was the obligatory apprenticeship for his certain career as a director.

He went about his stage-managing chores, but he was uneasy because of the gnawing worry about Marc's strange preoccupation.

4

Passions Spin the Plot

Ellen Everhope and Sinclair Turner strolled in. She cheerily asked if they were the first to return. Davis greeted them with an unctuous, gracious charm that made Uriah Heep seem like Robespierre passing judgment on Danton. But Sam was not placated by nor sympathetic with the producer's complaints the latter saw his scowl and asked him to join him up front in the box office from where they would try to get Bobby Francis on the phone. "What a blessing, unlimited local phone calls."

Sinclair quietly appraised Ellen when they were alone How fresh, wholesome, unspoiled she seemed to him. He wondered if she was still a virgin. He wondered how far he could get during the two weeks he'd be at the theater. I things work out, who knows, he might stay on for a few more weeks. He took up her question and answered, "Yes, we are the first. No dramatic entrance after the others are assembled."

She pouted in puzzlement and asked if actors must always be so calculating. He assured her that not all of them were Some had a cocky confidence about their talent that under al circumstances their quality, what the Greeks called *arete*, made anything they do stand out. This was true of many people in public life who were, really unconsciously, being actors without being aware of their great endowment. "Take yourself, for instance," he started to say.

"Now, now Mr. Turner . . ."

"Friends call me Sinclair, Ellen."

They smiled at each other and shook hands as though to seal a secret pact. He told her he was impatient to know all about her before he read her bio in the theater program. She diffidently capsulized her recent past for him: since college, "Oberlin," she answered his questioning eyebrows, and a few months of making the rounds among theatrical agents, she studied for a year at the Neighborhood Playhouse. She knew Joseph G. Heywood Jr. from his aborted career there; he had attended for less than a month. And that's where she met Sam, when he used to come backstage after the showcase productions. Sinclair retorted that he thought Sam was an uncle or guardian the way he told her what to do, more than is required or expected from a mere stage manager.

She assured him that she and Sam were just good friends. They'd gotten to know each other better a couple of summers back when she thought that she'd try a writing career and attended a writer's course at the University of Iowa where Sam was taking his master's degree. Sinclair interrupted her recital with a wry comment about all these brains in the theater, and how perhaps his day had passed. She quickly reproved him with her conviction there was no substitute for talent: after all, Duse, Barrymore, why, even Shakespeare never went to college. And just look at all the years of experience Sinclair has had. He hastened to say not so many years, at which they both laughed.

Ellen concluded by telling him of a few brief appearances in TV commercials and some summer stock in Pennsylvania. But they were only her start, maybe she would get experience in a variety of roles, of course nothing as wonderful as the variety he had played, for she had seen him in the movies, on TV, and on the stage—it was in Chicago when he was touring with a revival of *The Barretts of Wimpole Street*.

At that point she paused, and he sadly remarked that the *Barretts* was the last play he was in before his forced retirement due to Everett Scott's attempt at murdering him. She quickly, admiringly, enthusiastically told him how brave as well as forgiving he was to consent to relive the horrible episode again just to face the pistol again—she could not do it, she finished with a shudder.

If he were to make any time with her, this was his cue to elicit her sympathy, get her emotionally concerned for him. Therefore, his voice seemed anguished when he recalled the maniacal look in Scott's eyes when he aimed the gun at him. He sighed as he told her how frequently he'd awaken from a nightmare, hounded by that crazy look. He ruefully said he had not wanted Scott arrested, and the publicity of the trial had not helped any of them. At this she interrupted with the thought that bad publicity sometimes helped one's career look at the actors who were arrested for a drug rap and then went on to greater popularity and bigger box office attraction.

He shrugged off this suggestion by telling her that no one believed that he was innocent of any designs on Valerie. And Scotty had never gotten over his insane jealousy. Who knows he's apt to do anything yet. However, Sinclair assured her there never was any basis for Scott's jealous suspicions. She impulsively reached out her hand to him, which he grasped a he tenderly thanked her for chatting with him. Alas, he had lost so many of his so-called friends at that time, he told her and then weakly said how very lonesome it had been.

Now, don't overdo it, Sinclair old boy, he told himself don't push it too much. With a noble gesture of tossing his head as he released her hand, he urged her to go on about herself. There wasn't much more to tell. Sam had arranged an audition for her with Vergil Davis, and here she was.

And here they were, he beamed. He was so happy that the would be working together. He liked her quality. He'd see many actresses, but Ellen had a special quality, he assured her. She responded how pleased she was that they have scene together. Yes, he told her, a lovely scene. It could be one of the most memorable in the play if they worked on i together after Marc had blocked out the scene. It would be unprofessional to improvise any action in conflict with the director's concept. But by rehearsing privately together, they could intensify the meaning. He suggested that perhaps they could start that very night.

Her hesitation to consent, she explained, was because she had planned to memorize her lines that night. That would be perfect, he assured her, for they could learn the lines and the stage business while they cued one another. Before she could answer, he rose and drew her up with him.

"Toward the end of our scene, just before I carry you to the bedroom," he started with a most matter-of-fact, businesslike voice, "oh yes, let me see, that would be these chairs up right. Now, the mood must be poetic, and yet with a rapturous, exultant buildup, almost like a dance, a sensual rhythm as we respond to each other's excitement .."

Thus speaking and holding the script in one hand, he started acting the scene.

"As we stand at the window and I describe the mournful croak of the gulls over the misty river, you lose yourself in reverie, like so .."

He encouraged her to lean into his arms.

"You dreamily lean against me. As I say, 'Secluded in our temporary abode we seek...' I pause, groping for the right word, you turn to face me, to encourage me, and I take you in my arms like so..."

Loud applause from the darkened theater startled them, and they broke away from each other. Sam Dobrow came down the aisle toward the stage. As he jumped up onto the apron, with a faltering laugh Ellen told him they were starting to rehearse their scene together. Although he glowered at Turner, the stage manager spoke to Ellen and suggested she first allow the director to block out the scene. Turner countered by telling him that the director does not create the role, especially a role in which the actor is cast to play himself.

Sam disdainfully turned to him with, "I'm simply making a

professional suggestion to Miss Everhope."

"Professionally, you take care of your job and I'll handle mine."

Sam quietly assured him that that was exactly what he was doing. Ellen was baffled, and this made her belligerent. She wanted to scream at her self-appointed protector; instead, she coldly said, "This is silly. Mr. Turner and I . . . Sinclair and I were simply rehearsing in order to get the sense, the feel, the mood . . . and I don't see how it concerns you!"

Sam wanted to . . . oh, he didn't know what he wanted at that moment. He wanted both to spank her and to beseech her to understand his love for her. Instead, he calmly said, "It does concern me. Everything you do concerns me."

Ah, the brash arrogance of the creature. "That's ridiculous. So you helped me get this job. I'm deeply grateful. But the contract does not tie me down to breathe only when Sam Dobrow tells me to." She ran, fled out toward the steps and down to her dressing room.

Fool, fool, fool that you are, Sam. Hurry, run after her. You'll find her weeping by herself. That will be your cue to take her in your arms and comfort her. Instead, he remained for a confrontation with his new rival.

"What spirit! She's going to be a great actress, a star among stars. She's got extraordinary, quality, talent, fire . . ."

"Look here, Turner. She's not for you, so you better get that damn straight. Just stay away."

"Who the hell do you think you are . . ."

"I know more about you than you think. Women have been kind to you, too many women, too many kinds, and too kind. If you need new thrills, stick with your new toy, Joseph G Heywood, Jr. You can't corrupt him any more than he is. But stay away from Ellen . . . and stay away from any decent kid . . ."

As they glared at each other, they did not see the troupe enter; he was carrying a small, black bag.

Sinclair fumed, "You miserable, jealous son-of-a-bitch..."
"I'm warning you to lay off, Turner. If you don't I'll kill you. And I won't miss like Scotty did. I got a marksmanship medal in the army. I mean it—I'll kill you."
Sinclair Turner was silent, too silent as he looked behind Sam. Sam became aware that the actor was staring at someone. When Sam turned around he saw the trooper.
"Hi. We're just rehearsing."
The trooper's puzzled face took on a grin. "I'm in a hurry. Dr. Strong forgot his bag in my prowl car. Will you see that he gets it?"
The doctor must have wandered off somewhere, or else the trooper would have seen him outside. The stage manager was first inclined to tell the trooper to find Dr. Strong outside, but he reflected that in summer stock one must try to accommodate everyone in the community when possible. So he told the trooper to drop it on a chair as he smiled his assurance that the bag would be delivered.

Turner had moved away and stood with quiet dignity in the background as though he were oblivious to their conversation. The trooper thanked Sam as he quickly left. Ignoring Turner, Sam walked toward the opposite door and called, "Hey Doc. Doctor Strong..." Hearing no response, Sam went out the door in search of the doctor.

The moment the stage manager was out the door, Turner hurried to it and closed it. Then he quickly rushed to the little black bag and searched through it. Apparently he found what he wanted, swiftly hid it in his pocket, hurriedly closed the bag, and with assumed casualness took up his script, which he perused while he strolled about the stage, making certain to be as far from the bag as possible.

Joseph Jr. came in with a guilty and distressed look on his face. He eagerly asked Turner, "Am I late? Where is everyone?"

Sinclair Turner assured him that he was not late. Turner

walked to the door from where Joseph had entered, made certain no one was in sight, and then turned to Joseph. "Were you to the post office?"

"Yes. Nothing. But there's no reason for you to worry. My father keeps his promises. The money is sure to come by tomorrow."

"Well, it better be by tomorrow."

"But what'll I do until then? I can't wait. Dammit, you know that!"

Joseph's voice was almost hysterical. Turner looked apprehensively toward the door. "I don't grow the stuff. What in hell do you think I am? I've got to pay for it myself."

"I don't care..." Joseph's voice was almost a scream. Turner grabbed him by the arm.

"Are you crazy, damn you? Lucky for you, I came across a bonanza. Come on, let's get the hell out of here, down to my dressing room. Let's go."

5

From the Top

An onlooker, accustomed to the frenetic, feverish activity onstage during preproduction time, would be puzzled by the prevailing quiet when opening night is less than a week away and the stage business has not been blocked by the director. The calm at this theater was generated by the professionally businesslike authority with which Sam Dobrow handled his job as stage manager. The inevitable crisis every hour on the hour in summer stock never fazed his equanimity. He returned with Dr. Strong, who claimed his bag and then sat in the wings, and consulted his floor plan on his work table on the right corner of the stage's apron. Then the otherwise amiable stage manager exploded with some unusual curse words.

Before Dr. Strong could inquire about the cause of the outburst or offer any soothing words, Marilyn entered with Bobby Francis, the stage designer. Marilyn cheerfully announced the success of her mission to find the Yale man, nor was her air of triumph diminished when Sam waved her away and turned upon Bobby Francis with a cold fury.

"Denis said you'd have a model of the set, or didn't they teach you how to make one at... what's the name of that so-called school you attended? Oh yes, Yale."

"Verrry funny. You might try to hide your jealousy. However, I suppose all educationally deprived can't help being

39

envious. As for the model, no sweat. You'll have it tonight. What's the panic now?"

Sam slowly, witheringly looked at the effiminate-looking dandy and wanted to demolish him with a taunt about his epicene simpering. Suddenly Sam despised himself for his own lack of understanding. He knew that his impatience was not sparked by his desire for professional efficiency but by his lingering outrage against Sinclair Turner. Therefore, he became businesslike, pointed to the ground plan, and demanded that Bobby explain why the sight lines were askew and failed to reconcile themselves with the audience's seating. Bobby agreed that they were off and that he would correct them. Then Sam pointed to a cluttered "break" and asserted that it would interfere with stage business and ruin the actors' movement that Marc Denis had blocked.

Bobby Francis became shrill. "I refuse to have a box set."

Sam thought about this. Yes, there had to be a dynamic symmetry. But there would have to be accommodation to the director's concept. Before Sam could point out to Bobby the need for him to consult the director, Marilyn rushed into the discussion.

"Why don't you like boxes?"

"I'm not here to explain. I'm here to do nine shows, get nine pictures and nine program credits to show in New York, and that's all."

The imp gleefully attacked, "Your aversion to the box, an obvious Freudian symbol, is evidence of latent antifeminism. You don't like girls... and you know what that means..."

Sam groaned. And this was only the first day of the summer! "Listen Freud, this is a theater and not a psycho clinic. From now on, no more Freud! No more of your amateur psycho lingo! One more uncalled for piece of psychiatric bull from you, and out you go. Now, hand me the tape."

In her Lilith-like way, Marilyn grinned and conformed. She repressed the inclination to comment that she was a mother figure, umbilical symbol and all with the tape in her

From the Top

hand stretched out toward Bobby. She hovered over the stage manager and the set designer as she exercised extreme self-control in her compulsion to help them resolve the staging problems. When they were confronted by an impasse, she finally suggested they seek out Marc Denis at the diner and have him solve the problem. They grinned at each other in acknowledgment that the problem could be dumped in Marc's lap. After some corny banter of "It's your ship" from Sam to Marilyn and her response with an "aye, aye, Sir," the two men left Marilyn alone with Dr. Strong. She had not been aware of him.

"Hello. I'm Marilyn Samson."

"I'm Mitchell Strong."

When she asked him if he was one of the actors, he informed her that he was one of the apprentices. They both giggled as Marilyn said, "Shake, that makes two of us." When he asked her if she was to act in the play, she drew herself up and informed him that she was interested only in the technical end of the theater. Fortunately for Dr. Strong, when she started to explain her disinterest in acting, "because it's a narcissistic stage I left long ago," Everett Scott came through the stage door.

After Marilyn introduced the two men to each other, Everett said that he had spent the past fifteen minutes walking along the river. The doctor's customary diffidence could not conceal his enthusiasm for the countryside. Everett agreed that it was lovely country, still unspoiled by housing subdivisions. He had always dreamed of finding a refuge in such a peaceful, pastoral paradise. For he had memories of the Merrimac Valley. Dr. Strong observed that the Merrimac waters flow low and lazy at that time of the year.

Valerie had entered, had seated herself unobtrusively in a seat in the house, and had allowed herself the reverie of the bucolic idyll the two men evoked of a peaceful countryside interrupted by the terrifying spring floods that "have been known to rise ... up to the apron of this stage."

When Everett spoke of his coming here, of it being like a pilgrimage to his past, of his feelings of being immersed in timeless time, even before he was born, she wanted to take him in her arms and comfort him, wipe away her own anguish as she soothed his turbulent spirit that nostaligically spoke of this America. For their lives had been patterned like those of the busy millions, even at that moment, who hurried from factories and offices up and down the Atlantic coast to snatch their hectic lunch and then back to a soul-devouring routine. She reflected that perhaps there was some meaning to that life too, for in the routine they had no time to torture themselves in corrosive contemplation of lives constricted by the demands of nothing beyond their creature needs. And as the sun hurried westward, hour by hour the routine would be repeated in the time zones of the Mississippi, the Rockies, and then the West Coast, finally fleeing beyond the Pacific, only to come inevitably, relentlessly, day after day until the grave.

She heard Scotty's voice, as though he were in a trance, telling of the peace he found in the fleeting, elusive minutes along the river, of the spires of two churches that rose above the treetops. He had been born and brought up in a similar New England village, he said. For a brief moment he felt as though he had never left that spot by the river, the scene of brave dreams and baffling torments, of heartsickness and hunger, of a oneness with the honest earth alongside the river that flowed like the flowing of his life... and as the river surged with the floods, so did his life.

Alas, that was her Scotty all right! He certainly had not changed. She recalled how absolutely bathetically he rhapsodized about the earthiness, the simple life of the farmers in Indiana when they both drove westward from a one-night stand in Evansville. When he reproached her for her insensitivity because she had said his ecstasy was like the irridescent, fragile, lovely, exquisite golden strands of horseshit, he then actually did giggle; it was the one time she remembered he had the maturity to laugh at himself. But perhaps that quality in him, his romanticizing about America and the unquenchable pioneer spirit in it, was what endeared him to her—the unspoiled young American.

Her reverie was interrupted by Marilyn's crude and all-too-obviously puerile and smart-aleck observation that Everett was simply displaying an unconscious desire to crawl back into the womb. When Marilyn fled from Everett's impatient explosion, she saw Valerie, whereupon the irrepressible imp sought to redeem herself in the social amenities by introducing Dr. Strong to Valerie and to Sinclair Turner; the latter had returned during Everett's chat with the doctor.

Sinclair Turner turned to the doctor and observed how unsatisfying his lunch had been and asked if there were any good restaurants in the area. When Dr. Strong suggested the Blue Goose, Marilyn eagerly offered her judgment, for she had "dined there last night. It's for school teachers—the specialty of the house is doilies. Not for me, I love to eat. Maybe I was weaned too soon."

Everett left the brat to Dr. Strong who entered into a debate with her about whether her eating was compulsive or compensatory. He sought out Valerie in the quiet and dimness of the auditorium. His "How are you, Valerie?" was first answered by a wan and tolerant smile, then followed by a shrug and "No different from this morning."

The awkward silence was relieved by the distraction of Joseph's entrance and by their watching him edge his way toward Sinclair. Everett turned a few times toward the expectant Valerie, but each time he turned away with a sigh so that she wanted to scream at him. Then she reflected that the situation was most awkward for him and that she should help "break the ice"; she had promised Marc and Vergil that she'd be the good trooper. But why in hell must it be she! When, oh when would Scotty grow up! Finally, she, too, sighed and turned to him with "what have you been doing?" When he looked at her and asked "Since?" she silently nodded.

Everett's uncertain groping for an answer again convinced

Valerie that an actor should be forbidden—there ought to be a law—ever to open his mouth unless he had a script in front of him from which to read. How often she had spent dreary hours with her colleagues whose horizons reached only as far as the spotlights. Why, even the sun when it rose was only a spotlight for the actor. I'm only bitchy because I'm so uncertain, she thought. She had been reproaching herself for having consented to this bizarre gambit of appearing in "the true life story" of a theatrical scandal. She knew that she would end up despising herself if she didn't carry it off graciously. So she dismissed her doubts, her bitchiness, her resentments, and her impatience and turned to Everett with an encouraging smile. For all his grown-up, robust, and manly appearance, he was like a bashful boy with her now. She resisted the impulse to reach out her hand to comfort him with her touch. Would she ever touch him again? Before she could dwell on their lost intimacies, he had started to talk.

What had he been doing, he reflected. He smiled at her tentatively as though imploring her understanding. For him it was a disconcerting question. Sometimes he feared meeting his old friends, dreaded that they would ask the inevitable question. For crissakes, time doesn't stand still, and the years, few or many, are supposed to have built up equity for one's dreams, like some cumulative trust fund. And when the dread question is put to one by the dear friend of years ago— hell, it could even be a vaguely remembered acquaintance asking "What's with you?"—is one to submit clippings as one does a resume to a casting director or for the bio in a program? Oh yes, this friend is the kind who would be interested—nay, impressed—with a bank book or other evidence of success, or maybe a vita, a press notice of how you wowed thim in Pittsburgh, or some kind of medal. Would he turn down his lips and raise an eyebrow in derision if you reported anything less than a prideful, "Didn't you know, I'm the one who developed penicillin."

As Valerie shook her head quietly, indulgently, even understandingly, Scotty hastened on to suggest that he might say, "I've matured some, I think, in the years since I've seen you." He shrugged his shoulders as he suggested that the friend would peer closely at the thinned, greying hair, smile vacantly, and charitably escape to a quickly remembered, spurious luncheon conference. He cynically tossed up his arms with the query, "So, what can I say to you? I've matured some." He did not have to follow it with his intense assertion that his everlasting discontent obsessed him, for she knew and shared it.

It was not the time nor place to probe each other's depths, so Valerie matter-of-factly recounted to him her activities during the past few years: she had tried writing and only succeeded with an advertising agency: she had traveled, did a few roles in London. He countered with appearances in industrial shows, radio, TV, and a few road companies. But it was not the professional activity of his that interested Valerie. She wanted to know, simply, if he had ever thought of her, had ever missed her, had ever wanted to see her as she had unceasingly wanted him. She wondered if she should take her cue from the morning's reading and Sinclair's crude question—what did he really say after she left the last time? Instead they complimented each other on their professionalism and maturity in consenting to play themselves in a play that brazenly exploited their personal drama.

Meanwhile, Joseph, who had emerged from the passage leading down to the dressing rooms, was engaged in a melodramatic encounter with Sinclair Turner, made all the more ominous by their obvious efforts to keep aloof from the others while each appeared ready to kill the other. Had any of the others overheard the bitter recriminations between the two, he would have been mystified by the threats of Sinclair to cut off Joseph without something or other and then Sinclair's pleading and assurance to Joseph that he was devoting his life to the young man's career. The glassy-eyed Joseph retorted with a taunt that they needed each other. It ended with

Joseph's promise that his parents would come across—"they better, if they know what's good for them"—and that Sinclair better be sure to come across with "the stuff." Further discussion was interrupted by the return of Marc, Dobrow, and Bobby.

When the actors alertly approached the stage, Marc waved them back with a smile and a promise that he'd be with them directly. He picked up the ground plan from Sam's table, surveyed the stage, looked out into the house, and quickly snapped out his decision: "O.K., Bobby, rake it in. Remember the scrim and the change—we have no grid and we can't fly the set. Don't rake too much, I can work in front of the furniture. Make a note, Sam, for an extra couple of baby spots on number three for the apron."

Marilyn made the notes as Sam, biting into his hamburger and sipping coffee, nodded agreement to Marc, who continued, "Chalk it now, Sam, and tape tonight after Bobby gets the revised plan to you ..." He turned and glowered at Bobby, "... and the model. And that's to be at 4:30 sharp. Now, where's my script?"

When Sam handed Marc the only script on his table, Marc asked where the stage manager's script was. Sam told him that he had given it to Dr. Strong, who might read the judge's part, and then he introduced the doctor and the director to each other. Marc said that he would read him for the role when the afternoon's rehearsal broke, around 4:15. As the doctor handed back the script to the stage manager, he asked if he could hang around and help. Marc consented and then called out, "Places, everybody. We start at the top."

As Marc arranged himself at one of the seats at the stage manager's table, where he would do little sitting, Dobrow walked about the stage and pointed out the area to the assembled company. He explained that exit right was down two-thirds, and pointed to two chairs that stood sentinels there. Exit left was up left near rear wall. Scrim will mask Sinclair's room where the tape on the floor indicated. Window was up right of fireplace, also indicated by a couple of chairs. Trophies, pictures in uniform, helmet, scroll, pistol on hook, all over fireplace. Entrance to Sinclair's room right of center as indicated by two chairs. In front of scrim, Valerie's room. In it, sofa—indicated by three chairs, phone on table down left.

After having indicated the set, after the actors had noted it all in their respective scripts, after Sam had answered a few questions to clarify some points, he seated himself alongside Marc at his stage manager's table.

Sam announced, "Places. Curtain. Count three, then Brnng, Brnng, Brnng."

Marc referred to his script, "Valerie, you enter on the third ring. Once again Sam. And mark it."

Sam repeated the Brnngs; Valerie entered and rushed to the phone, picked it up—and the first rehearsal began.

6

The Blocking

Except for that damned, mysterious letter in his pocket, Marc had reason to be pleased with the rehearsal that afternoon. There is nothing like working with professionals, he thought. They repeated each of his instructions as they marked their scripts and walked through each movement, each turn, each entrance and exit, each gesture, each turn of the head, each time they sat or rose, and each time they used a prop. Marc cautiously refrained from suggesting "line readings," the inflection and interpretation of any speech, for he knew how touchy actors were when they were exposed to criticism of their interpretations publicly. He would have found it difficult to decide which of his three principals was most responsive: Valerie quietly and diffidently went through her paces; Everett was tentative and muttered to himself as he repeated the blocking and jotted on his script; Sinclair was briskly silent, even anticipating Marc's instructions. The stage manager could not have been more alert.

The smoothness of the rehearsal might have been a happy augury for an unusual production, for a play that would wow the first-night audience and launch the season and, Marc hoped, a new play on its way to success in New York, if it were not for Joseph G. Heywood, Jr. who walked as though in a daze. He dropped his script innumerable times, he forgot his cues, he bumped into the chairs that marked the furniture, he

The Blocking

obliged Marc to repeat his directions. Marc had an uneasy, disheartening foreboding. Why in hell had he consented to casting the boy in the play? Vergil had breezily told him not to worry as he observed that almost everyone who came to the box office asked if he was really the son of the famous Hollywood "Little Napoleon."

Sam's quiet but authoritative voice called Marc back to the moment. The stage manager called "places everybody," and then "curtain." Marc saw Sinclair enter, pretend he was closing a door, and then read his markings on the script: "I come through door right, like so." He interrupted to ask Sam if that was the bedroom door. The stage manager nodded a response. Sinclair barked at him, "Speak up, man. I asked you if that was the bedroom door." Unperturbed, with a quiet and colorless voice, Sam replied, "One, it is the bedroom door, and two, I indicated all entrances before we started the scene."

When Sinclair Turner appeared to be about to retort, Marc interrupted with a businesslike snap, "Go back, start with your entrance again, Sinclair."

Again Sinclair Turner walked through his directions for the scene as he had marked it from Marc's direction. "After I come through the bedroom door, I cross to the fireplace and adjust my picture on the mantelpiece, then I cross left, select and set record in the hi-fi, listen to the music for a moment, check the glasses and ice on the bar, then pick up a magazine and sit on the couch."

At that point, Marc interrupted with instructions to Sam to mark his master script with a sight cue, when Sinclair opened the magazine after he was seated, the stage manager was to ring the doorbell. Just as they were ready to run through it, Marc stopped them. He was unhappy with the obviously contrived moment for the bell, it lacked spontaneity. All of them patiently waited while Marc lit a cigarette and paced about. Soon, he turned to them with, "Let's reverse it. Sinclair, at the rise you are seated, looking through the magazine. Look at your wrist watch. Then go through the business of the picture, glasses and ice, all the time giving the feeling of impatience and anticipation. Change the record. The bell will ring on the sound cue of three bars of music after Sinclair has changed the record. Sam, make a note to select some schmaltzy records."

Looking up from his script on which he was busily jotting down the new stage business, Sinclair said, "I should think I would select the music. After all, it's my taste we are portraying—I never listen to 'schmaltzy' music."

Sam disgustedly threw down his pencil and turned to Marc as he muttered something about who in hell does he think he is, some character in a Pirandello play? He'll next want to write his own dialogue. But Marc only grinned and nodded to Sinclair, "You've got a good point there. See Sam after the break and give him a few titles you'd like. Then, Sam, you clear it with me." Then he quietly turned to Sam, "Save it for the big crises when they come, buddy."

They quickly started the scene again. Sam indicated to Sinclair that there would be two rings. Sinclair went through the stage business, and after he had changed the record he hummed three bars of Stravinsky's "Firebird" at which point the stage manager came in with his Brnng, Brnng, whereupon the actor moved to the chairs designated as the outside door, went through the dumb show of opening a door, and Valerie walked through into the room.

Sinclair read from his script, *"Hello. I've been expecting you. Come right in."*

Valerie responded from her script, *"What a sweet little place."*

Sinclair: *"An ill-mannered thing but mine own."* He then removed her coat.

Valerie interrupted to observe that her script said that she takes off her own coat. Marc agreed and had her make her entrance again.

Then Sinclair read, *"Let me take your coat."*

"Thank you, but I'll just drop it on the chair." Then she turned to Marc, "Which chair?"

Marc instructed her as he pointed to Sam to mark it "Up right, beyond the window on the other side of the fireplace."

Valerie marked it in her script and then continued, "I cross up right, drop my coat on chair, I'm taking off my coat as I cross, then cross down, stop at fireplace to admire the picture and say, 'My, you're quite a handsome figure in uniform.'"

Sinclair came in on cue, "Thank you."

"And these things?" Valerie made motions as though she were handling some objects, "I pick up the gun and the helmet."

"Trophies from Germany."

"How exciting. I'd love to hear all about it some day."

"Not much to tell. No heroics. I can tell you in one brief sentence. I was with a U.S.O. troupe."

"Scotty's expecting me home soon. I haven't much time. Let's get to the script."

Sinclair moved away from her, "'I was reading it in bed. I'll get it.' I cross right and go through the door like so."

Valerie crossed to the hi-fi, "I go to the hi-fi, turn off the record. Cross down to the sofa, sit, put on my glasses, take script out of my purse . . . "

Marc interrupted her, "Change that. Sit down first, put on glasses, look at script, become aware of music, rise and cross to the hi-fi, turn off record. That's your sound cue to return, Sinclair. Got it Sam? O.K. everybody. Now walk it."

Valerie walked through the scene, reading her stage business between her dialogue, and Sinclair entered on cue. The dialogue provided for her to explain that she had turned off the music, and Sinclair graciously offered a drink from the bar. Valerie crossed from the hi-fi to the sofa and asked Marc on which end of the sofa to sit. He instructed her to sit on the left and suggested that she maintain a businesslike attitude, for she came to read the scene and nothing more. After Valerie refused the drink and was seated, Sinclair read from his script.

"*I was thinking we might start with the scene where you are on the sofa just before we dance. We can go through the dance bit, the breaking of the unicorn, and so on up to Amanda's entrance. Then we'll go back to where I offer you the dandelion wine.*"

Valerie responded on cue with her "*All right.*" Then they read the roles of Laura and the Gentleman Caller from Tennessee Williams's *Glass Menagerie*. The rehearsal continued until they were about to dance. Sinclair read the lines, "*A little higher. Right. Now don't tighten up, that's the main thing about it—relax.*"

Valerie laughed, "*It's hard not to.*" She tried to pull away from him. He held her tighter. Her laughter started to get hysterical as she struggled to break away.

Sinclair dropped his script in his puzzlement as he asked, "What's this?"

Valerie was now sobbing, and Marc hurried over to her as she slumped into a chair. He both tried to comfort her and to insist she behave. She sobbed more loudly, "I can't go on with it. I know you'll all hate me. I never should have agreed. I need the job . . . I need . . . I . . . oh, I just want to die . . ."

Marc turned to the company with, "Ten minute break, everybody."

Sinclair approached Valerie in an effort to help, "Now Valerie . . . "

She jumped up with a scream, "No! Leave me alone . . . !" Then she ran out of the theater.

Like frightened chicks who run to their mother hen, the baffled actors turned in bewilderment to Marc; he simply sat with a blank stare that he interrupted only to relight a cigarette. Sam thought, okay Marc, here's your crisis; how're you gonna handle this one? The silence seemed interminable. Sinclair Turner finally blurted out, "What got into her?"

"That's not hard to answer," Everett Scott spoke quietly and deliberately. "The idea of you touching her was enough . . ."

"Who the hell do you think you're talking to, you creep . . . " Sinclair Turner advanced toward Scott.

"Too bad I didn't kill you. Next time I won't miss. I'll kill you . . ."

Before the two could grapple with each other, Sam and Marc were between them. They didn't see Davis come running down the isle until he was at the foot of the stage and screaming, "What's going on here?"

Sinclair turned down stage and shouted at Davis, "I don't have to put with this punk. He's threatened my life, and no contract can keep me here under such conditions. I'm through." With this, Sinclair Turner jumped down alongside Davis and walked proudly up the aisle and out of the theater through the front of the house.

7

Between the Lines

Davis tried to chase after him, then thought better of it and ran up on the stage where he authoritatively demanded, "Will someone tell me what's going on here?" No one answered him, but Marc turned to Scott.

"Scotty, I'm counting on you. Go after Valerie and get her back. I'll handle Sinclair all right."

Everett Scott hurried out after Valerie. Marc took Davis aside and explained what had happened. Davis slapped his forehead in disappointment. "Just my luck! Why didn't we have a reporter present for it? Wow, what a publicity scoop this would have been!"

The director looked at him and shook his head slowly "To each his own. That's all this means to you?"

"Don't worry about Valerie. She'll come around."

"You know all the answers, huh? You're dealing with human beings ..."

"Human beings my ass. I know them better than you do. I've been around a long time, and I know actors. When it comes to figure what's human, forget about actors."

"But they're not just actors, and this isn't only a play we're rehearsing. You're capitalizing on their sensational trial ... so, O.K. But these three haven't seen each other since it happened until this morning. You can't expect them to be puppets and just read lines. It's their own lives they're reenacting. Valerie is a decent human being ..."

me, everyone has faith in each other. This production will be one big, fucking revival meeting. And I'll remain Mr. Anonymous author."

Perhaps, who knows, thought Davis, I might have been like that. There was a time when he got out of college when he had been determined to devote his life to a poet's theater. That was the time he and Marc had really been close. But the world was real and had to be faced every minute of the day. To hell with it. Why dig it up. There's a play to get on, and if Marc insists on living in the past, let him.

Marc must have read his thoughts as he continued, "My son is the future. The pendulum will swing, and my son must build it with honest straw as must all the decent people...."

"You sound like you're enacting a role in a play from the 1930s. We got ourselves a play to put on now. By the way, if it's any comfort to you, Sinclair Turner turned me down when I first offered him the role. But when he heard you were going to direct, he almost got down on his hands and knees to beg for the part. Go figure that out."

That indeed was odd. If anyone had a reason to stay away from him, Marc reflected, it was Sinclair Turner. When Marc caught him trying to seduce a sixteen-year-old starlet, he had Sinclair thrown off the lot. The actor had sworn to get even. Now, why should Sinclair have so desperately wanted to get into a play directed by Marc? His speculations were interrupted by Dobrow, who came onstage and immediately got into a hassle with the producer.

The point at issue was the failure of the technical man to arrive. Davis assured the stage manager that the technical man, from Carnegie Tech who had worked in summer stock in the Poconos, was sure to arrive that night. Dobrow asked, "Worked in summer stock? As what?" Before Davis could answer the sneer, Bobby came in with a request for Davis's car; he had to get to town to pick up some chintz.

Davis, too, had to get to town. "Give me the sample. I'll pick it up. Just tell me the yardage. You stay here and finish what you have to do with Dobrow."

At that point, Sinclair Turner appeared. With surprising calm, he came down the aisle and handed Davis a piece of paper and said, "I suggest you get a couple of records of Noel Coward. His is my type of sophisticated music for my scenes."

Having said that, he quietly and with swaggering dignity walked toward the stairs and exited down to his dressing room while Marc grinned his approval to Davis.

Davis saw Marilyn come on stage. "You ... you'll come with me and sit in the car in case I can't find a parking spot. And ..."

Everett Scott came running in. "I couldn't find her."

Davis was stunned for but a moment. He whirled to Marc. "Come with me, please Marc. We've got to find her—otherwise there's no play and we'll be sunk."

The two of them rushed out.

Bobby turned to Sam, "It's going to be one of those summers. Hysterical actors, hysterical producers—how do they get that way?"

Before Sam could retort, Marilyn volunteered, "It's their guilt complexes based on a sense of inadequacy. It all goes back to forced and premature toilet training." Sam wished that he would become immune to Marilyn's immature, pseudopsychological analyses—harmless and meaningless in themselves, but in this instance underlining the uncertain nature of actors and their lives.

8

Secondary Plot

Inquiries at the Widow Richard's house where Valerie was staying had resulted in the information that Valerie had borrowed the Widow's bicycle and gone off somewhere. That was a good sign, observed Marc, for if Valerie had intended to quit she would have packed up and been on her way to the bus or railroad station. What to do next? Should they go back into the car and drive up and down the country lanes in search of her? No, decided Vergil. He would assume that everything was status quo ante. Meanwhile he would get back to the theater and pick up Marilyn, while Marc could read Dr. Strong in the judge's role and otherwise hold the fort with the hope that Valerie may return. They left word with the Widow Richards to ask Valerie, when she returned, to wait for Davis, who wished to take her to dinner.

Davis now didn't seem to be too upset, for he merely said, "If I had the time I'd be able to work out a wow of a publicity deal on this. We need something with real punch to it. Have you any ideas?"

Marc had a wow of a punch in his pocket—the letter! Would its use as a publicity stunt solve the puzzle of what it was all about? He was certain that it would not. All it would do would be to reveal him to the mob with its lingering McCarthyite psychosis. As benign and decent as all the people seemed to be in the area, there was a hard-core enclave of reactionary, 100 percent Americans. Why, just a dozen miles away on the coast a village had made a cult out of the most notorious, self-proclaimed "patriot" who had again and again appeared as a paid informer before a congressional committee and who had capitalized on his role as a provocateur by authoring a book about his activities. Again Marc let pass the opportunity to disclose the letter to Vergil. He did, however, resolve to seek out the informer, who seemed to be so different from the decent stock in the area. But that gambit should be deferred until after the play will have opened, for if the self-appointed guardian of patriotism was indeed the author of the vicious letter, a visit by Marc before the opening night might really spur the creep on to some form of sabotage. And if he was not the author of the letter, then why give him any ideas?

On the way back to the theater, Marc reflected on the narrowness and the insularity of their lives, of their drives, of their preoccupations. They were facing a crisis, true. But how pitifully small and inconsequential were their concerns when measured alongside the cosmic turbulence of the world. He suddenly realized that he hadn't read a metropolitan newspaper in over two weeks. Was this play-acting world a fit occupation for grown-up men? Why, the simplest, elementary stage business, the crossing of the stage, the lifting of a prop, the painting of a doorjamb, all this minutiae that required routine common sense and no more had been pretentiously elevated to college courses in highfalutin college drama courses.

Despite his long history in the theater and films, Marc was always self-conscious when he fell into the pattern of lingo used on stage and on the lot, the special jargon of the specialists. He knew that he could always put on a most professional production with no more than the actors, the stage manager, the prop man, the costume person (if required), and the technician, in addition to the scene designer. For him the proliferation of featherbedding jobs was always an encumbrance. He always sneered at the highly funded groups when he saw their programs with assistant stage managers, script girl and assistant script girl, dialogue director, production assistant, ad nauseum. It reminded him of a discussion on TV between two people in front of a table with a starkly simple background. After the program, the list of credits, he once counted, came to sixty-five people!

It was all because of union rules. A political radical, a strong union man, Marc was uneasy about the turn his thoughts had taken. He knew of a highly talented young man who could not get into the stagehands union while the son of a long-time member got in easily. Marc argued with himself that the son of the owner of any business could step into his father's business, so why not the son of a worker in the stagehands union? He did not know the answer. But he did know that the waste was as bad as that in the army as he had known it, and the result was prohibitively mounting costs of production that will, must, destroy the creative theater.

Slowly the car turned a bend in the road and continued along the Merrimac River on their way back to the theater. This was Thoreau's river. And wasn't it Thoreau who had suggested that reading the newspaper was a waste of time, for it reported, month after month, ships lost at sea, men ensnarled with the law, conflagrations and controversies the world over—and months later the same melancholy news, only the names would be different.

Was he wrong in immersing himself so in life's little inconsequentialities? There was a time when he passionately knew that his way was so right. Perhaps he should not have left the theater, should not have succumbed to the blandishments of Hollywood. Even during the anguished cold-war years of the indecent McCarthy, there were oases of hope in the theater, there were brave writer, producers, and actors who dared defy the mass hysteria. Marc was about to make a mental vow that if this play succeeded he would never leave the theater again. He wryly smiled and dismissed the idea of a New Year's type of resolution, for he knew that once the pendulum would again swing, as it inevitably must, he would try to reach as wide an audience as possible with his "art." He audibly sighed at his own pretentiousness.

His companion turned for a moment from his driving with a "huh?" Marc quickly dissembled with a speculation about how the lovely countryside was doomed to progress, for it would soon be covered with houses for commuters to Boston, some fifty miles away. Davis agreed and suggested that the million dollars they'll make on the play be invested in acreage along the river. Marc welcomed the other's pragmatic outlook and entered with him into a discussion of investments and security. His own perversity impelled him sardonically to laugh at themselves for "sounding like a couple of old creeps ready to retire from life and worry only about their investment yields."

"When I was a kid at college, I said that the best thing that could happen to me when I reached 65," said Davis, "was to go broke. That would oblige me to start all over again—a challenge that would rejuvenate me."

"And now?"

"Oh boy, have I changed my mind! Security, pal, security."

Here he was back to the unresolved discussion he'd had with Davis: what security had the actor? Alas, Valerie, indeed, would be back just as he was back and would see this production through. What choice had they? Was Everett here, in the play, because he needed the security of employment? Marc would have liked to believe that Everett was in the play because he truly loved Valerie. Who knows, perhaps those two may yet be reconciled and make a go of it. Marc smiled to himself as he reflected upon his wish for the Hollywood ending. And how about Sinclair Turner? Perhaps Davis was right, perhaps Sinclair was the typical actor in search of a role, any role, especially this one, which would glamorize his own life. Marc resolved that he would try to know Sinclair better, try to find some redeeming feature in

Secondary Plot 65

the actor. Marc hated himself for bristling with an unhealthy antipathy of vague origin every time he thought of or encountered Sinclair.

Late that night, after Marc wearily and impatiently tossed onto the night table the master script of *Bus Stop*, which he was blocking for next week's rehearsal, he lay back in bed and reflected on the recurrent figure of the decadent, world-weary, morally maimed intellectual in each of Inge's plays. As a counterfoil, the dramatist always had the robust, earthy, unattached, all-male figure. Marc saw this as Inge's preoccupation as a writer who used his otherwise tightly constructed plots to explore the anomalous, tortuous predicament of the sensitive mind in its encounter with the raw brutality of life. He thought of Lee Perkins.

Underneath the obvious annoyance of Valerie's hysterics of that day, his own lingering uncertainties, his irritation with Vergil's aloofness from the human problems of the troupe, and the unresolved urgency of that confoundedly vicious letter was his uneasy compassion for Lee Perkins. Confident that Perkins's play would at least be a soporific to lull him to sleep and give him some respite from his gnawing problems, he picked up the play.

Forget about the letter he did, but sleep he did not. For the play was indeed exciting. At first, Marc was impatient with the demands of the verse in Alexandrine couplets upon his attention, for the style slowed the reading. Then it became apparent that the epic concept demanded poetic treatment. In the plot, Perkins had telescoped three world wars: World War I, World War II, and World War III. His device was simple and economical, for the setting was an isolated and forgotten dugout, a subterranean advance station in France in which were Allied soldiers and officers from World War I—all ghosts—waiting for contact, for some word of instructions from field headquarters. Into this scene, after unusual bombardment, crawl two American paratroopers from World War II. One is dead while the wounded other hovers between life and death. The ghosts believe them to be German spies, courtmartial them, and condemn them. The Americans plan an escape, aided by the ghost of a French girl who is with the others. In the last act, after a cataclysmic explosion, a dead woman and her two children, a boy and girl, crawl into the dugout. The horrendous hydrogen bombs had so disfigured the children that, although they are alive, they are frightful mutations. The rest of the human race had been destroyed by these Doomsday bombs, and the two mutations will go forth as the new Adam and Eve to spawn weird creatures of a new race.

The play, to which Perkins had given the title *Headless Victory*, a title organically derived from the content because one character in it was constantly sculpting out of the mud a replica of the Headless Victory of Samothrace he had seen at the Louvre, excited Marc. Of course, the play needed some more work of a minor kind. Some of the verse that was strained and contrived needed cleaning up.

The big problem was to get the play produced. Vergil would not, could not dare try it at this summer theater. Marc really admired Vergil for having dared to start his season with an unknown new play instead of the usual pabulum of recent Broadway hit comedies most producers fed their audiences on the summer circuit. Marc resolved to get the company excited about the play, infect them with his own enthusiasm so that later in the season they would rehearse it on their own time and then give a postseason production for a few nights. The last week of the season they would not be rehearsing and would be free from the pressure experienced all summer. Then they might bring it to New York for a showcase production at an off-Broadway house.

Happy and excited, Marc tried to sleep. Suddenly he sat up and looked at Perkins's last act again. It was typed in the script style just like that on the dread letter. His dismay did not

Secondary Plot 67

permit him to sleep. Could Perkins, in his resentment against theater people because he had been denied a hearing, be so vindictive as to have written the letter—and possibly, actually, intend harm? If not Perkins, surely not the pretty, harmless Delores in the box office? Who else had access to the typewriter? The letter was postmarked New York a week ago. There must be hundreds of like typewriters in New York.

Marc carefully scrutinized the letter and the typewritten last act to find oddities that were common to any of the letters of the alphabet that coincided with each other. He thought he did, but only under a magnifying glass, which he did not have, could he be certain. Suppose it was the same machine that had typed the play and the letter—how did the letter get to New York? Easy. Whoever typed it, if he or she did, in West Endicott could easily have had it remailed from New York through an accomplice. Could it have been his wife? What motive would she have? The same negative response to this albino kid, to Delores, and to Davis himself as the possible writers of the letter eliminated them. He decided to question Delores about the people who had used the typewriter. But first he'd have to find a magnifying glass in order to make certain there were similarities in the letter with the type of the machine. Ah, if only he dared go to the police.

Suppose it had been typed on the same machine in New York. Who had access to it in New York? It had always been on the small desk near the window in his son's room. His son lived with his mother, whom Marc had not seen in months. He understood how her despair, which fed on his inability to continue in films and his refusal to abandon that work which he was determined to pursue, had gradually led to their parting. She had been his great support, his conscience, his moral righteousness—at first. Then she had started a campaign of subtle suggestions that he get out of the field and work at some simple job so that they would lead a fruitful and uncomplicated life. His obstinate refusal brought her to an open campaign and constant attack. She had gotten a job and supported them. This undermined his self-confidence. Was he the all-American male who must be the head of the household? He could not root out the pattern of his existence, which had been formed by a lifetime of conditioning. He became suspicious of every word she uttered, words in which he suspected sneers at himself. She had been very noble and decent when he was constantly being harassed by governmental agents. Then he found each word and attitude of hers to be bitchy and bitter toward him. They had parted a half year ago. They were highly rational about it. Perhaps one day they would again make it together.

No, it could not have been his wife, for, what motive had she? There was nothing vindictive nor vicious in her.

If only he could go to the police and be sure that they would not call in the federal people . . .

Why not dismiss it all as the work of a crank? Why not tear up the letter and simply get along with the job of getting the play on, for the success of the play would bring a reconciliation with his wife, a new career in the theater, and possibly another chance in films? He believed in the pendulum theory of history—this, too, shall pass—the repressive years will yield to a rebirth of liberalism and decency when the public will, in revulsion against the indecencies of McCarthyism, again embrace the American ideal of fair play. But Marc tormented himself in speculating whether he was still wallowing in the sentimentality of the thirties when, as a high school kid he had subscribed to the affirmation of life, a life that promised a better tomorrow to be distilled out of the anguished days of the dismal Depression years.

Being mentally mired down in the past was not solving the problem of the letter. There must be something behind it, more to it. Suppose something tragic does occur, his silence will have made him an accessory. Then, should it come out that he had the dread warning, how could he explain to the police why he had remained silent? He would damn well tell them that he thought it to be the work of a crank, of some deranged excrescence of a discredited McCarthy era.

9

Private Lives

There was little time for much speculation and introspection the next few days. Valerie had been won back, rehearsals proceeded on schedule, Dr. Strong was a real find in the role of the judge and as assistant to the stage manager, for he knew just where and from whom to borrow the correct furniture and props from the townsfolk, Bobby Francis continued his epicene antics with an air of assurance that did not entirely dispel Dobrow's skepticism, while the actors conducted themselves with professional tidiness. Marc worried about Joseph. The youth always appeared to be in a trance, to forget his lines, and to be beyond Marc's earnest efforts to help him. Joseph seemed relaxed and actually smiled only when the irrepressible amateur Freudian, Marilyn, kept up her puerile, pseudo, psychiatric pronouncements.

The state trooper hung around the theater more than his duties warranted, thought Marc. At first he thought that Ellen was the attraction for the man. Other than casual banter and pleasantries, there was nothing to suggest a budding romance. It was apparent that the trooper was reveling in a glamorous contact with the "theater."

At times, Marc came to the conclusion that the trooper was getting quite friendly with Sinclair, when the latter was not in a huddle with Joseph. Those two seemed to be more and more isolated in a world of their own.

Marc mentally shook himself out of his concern. What was

he doing in being concerned about them? He had known so many groups to be destroyed for no reason other than the abrasive contact of people thrown together, people with their own personalities. He was determined not to allow himself to be dragged into their problems, determined not to imagine backstage intrigue and, above all, not to get involved with any if there was merely a hint of it. Despite his resolve, Marc worried and wondered about Joseph. He wished that the next ten days were over, and then, perhaps, the fraternization between Joseph and Sinclair would dissolve when Sinclair returned to New York. Wish the next ten days to be over! Marc dismissed such thinking with the realization that that was wishing his life away.

The elements of the set were starting to take shape. By midweek, early in the morning, Dobrow, Marilyn, Bobby, and Dr. Strong were busily hammering away at a flat as they adjusted it into place. Bobby actually wasn't involved in the work—he supervised. He held a container of coffee in his hand as he minced about with instructions to the others.

Be it on Broadway or anywhere across the nation, onstage or backstage, in dressing rooms or among the seats of the theater, empty coffee containers with doused cigarettes in them lie about in mute testimony of intense work by theater folk who have no time to go out for lunch, for a coffee break, or merely to relax. A fastidious housekeeper would go out of her mind with this litter. But in the *theater* it was part of the glamorous ambience amidst the intense artists. Bobby was not alone as he absentmindedly drank his coffee in between his instructions to the others. Sam had the others stand alongside a flat they held while he joined Bobby—Sam picked up his cardboard coffee cup en route—as they hopped off the stage apron into the house and discussed the rake of the flat to make certain that the sight lines were not violated.

A brisk and businesslike Davis came down from the front of the house and asked for Marc. Not finding him, he left instructions that all were to be on hand at 12:30 when the local radio-station people would be there to record a scene from the play and some chitchat with the company. He also instructed Sam that this routine would be followed every Wednesday for the remainder of the season for the play that would be in rehearsal for the ensuing week. Sam asked what scene. Davis advised him to tell Marc to pick one that would titillate the listeners and entice them to the theater. Oh yes, he remembered, Valerie Walker was to be available the next day for lunch as the guest of honor at the weekly Kiwanis luncheon. "Publicity and all that jazz."

Davis was congratulating himself on the smoothness of the operation when Dobrow called him aside, out of earshot of the others. The problem was young Joseph. The young actor had not been seen since before dinner the night before. He had not slept at his boarding house. When Davis tried to tell the stage manager not to worry, Sam turned on him.

"I hope you know what you're doing. That kid is a junky. You better know it and make arrangements for a stand-in for him."

Davis laughed above Dobrow's scowl. After all, didn't the kid's parents know him? They had assured him that the boy was solid stuff. Thanks to him, the advance at the box office was phenomenal. People come up and ask if he really is the son of Little Napoleon. When they are assured that he is, they buy and buy. Davis was tempted to carry over the play for an extra week instead of *Bus Stop* because of the presence of Joseph G. Heywood, Jr. Not only would he save money on new sets, on jobbing in new actors, but the receipts of the two weeks would be enough to carry the rest of the season. After all, he had some of his own money tied up in this venture, let alone his reputation. He quickly assured Sam that he put his own money into the company because of his absolute faith in the new play, in the town, in this theater that would become an institution of theater art for all the Northeast. Furthermore, Davis had asked a mature trouper to look out for Joseph—he had asked Sinclair Turner to take the young man under his wing.

"Wow! That's perfect! A junkie and a queer."
Davis whirled bitterly upon Dobrow. "Don't you go spreading such damned malicious gossip around here. You don't know this community. For chrissakes, that's all we need. They'll ride us out of town on a rail. Just keep your dirty trap shut and don't give out with such crap! And if these actors don't keep their noses clean, I'll get others. Actors are two for a nickel."

"And how about producers? What's the going rate?"

"I see, a wise guy. Alright, smart aleck, why didn't you organize this company, get the theater, hire the company, select the plays? What price would you put on enterprise, on the feel of the theater, on taste, on intuition, a knowledge for what the public may be ready to pay to see in the theater? Just you take care of your stage managing and dream your dreams of one day becoming a director—that's what all stage managers dream about. And, oh yes, you better understudy Joseph's role. In between times when you're writing your memoirs about the theater, be sure to write down a note with my instructions for Marc. Now piss off and don't bug me. I've got my job and you take care of yours."

After the producer left, Sam turned to his crew and appraised their work. The flats appeared to be satisfactorily in place. Except for doors, a window, and the fireplace, the room was taking shape. He detailed the others to the workshop in the adjacent barn where they were to get and bring back the flats for outside the doors.

As they filed out the door they passed Valerie, who exchanged "Good Mornings" with them. Sam gave her Davis's message about the luncheon with the Kiwanis. She greeted this with a groan, but quickly agreed with Sam as to its publicity value.

Alone on stage, Valerie took her script out of her tote bag and started to walk through her part. She did not see Everett enter. He silently stood near the door and watched her. Yes, he loved her—perhaps more than ever before, if that were possible. For a mature woman, how boyish her figure was. Her honey-colored hair was too long for the ponytail effect she wore, but he was so pleased to see how it gave him a full view of her sad, pale, heavenly face. She wore tight pants through which could be seen the elastic tightness of her very brief panties high up on her thighs. Her loose jersey sweater allowed her breasts to jiggle as she turned. As usual, he thought, no bra; she always was conscious that her breasts were no larger than those of a young girl first emerging into puberty. He recalled how he delighted in their firmness and responsive nipples. Ah, how he wanted to rush to her and crush her to him! He felt like a voyeur and was about to turn away and leave when she saw him.

"Good morning."

"Good morning. Are we the first?"

She told him that the crew had been there and had gone to the barn. He suppressed his urge to tell her how lovely she looked; instead he observed to her the enchantment of the morning and expressed a hope that Marc would rehearse outdoors today. She agreed and told him that she had taken a long walk.

"By yourself?"

She did not answer. He realized how stupid the question must seem to her. Should he explain that all he meant was that unless she preferred to walk with someone else—say Ellen—he would enjoy joining her. Instead, after an awkward pause, he said, "I'm sorry, I didn't mean to pry." She waved it aside with a distant "forget it." Again he knew that was not what he wanted to say. They turned from each other and concentrated on their scripts.

He could not concentrate. He had to talk with her. It had been so intolerably long since he had been with her. "I took a walk this morning too. Along the river. I'm very fond of it. I shall loathe leaving here."

"You know where the orchard is behind the Widow Richards's house?" He nodded. "I walked beyond it and found

the most peaceful pond. The water lillies were open."
His river view, he told her, was worth a visit. He offered one day to show it to her. She turned back, silently to her script. She had not rebuffed him for all her neutral, civil responses. And when will they be alone again? He imagined he was trembling with his eagerness to talk with her. Yet he was afraid. Even though he decided to keep silent, he heard himself, practically involuntarily, talking to her.

"I've been wanting to ask you—why did you accept this role?"

"Very simple. I needed the job."

"I offered you alimony."

"Please. I thought you understood."

There it was. He had hoped—what did he hope? He may as well face it. The reason he had taken the job . . .Before he could spell it out for himself, as though she had read his mind, she was asking, "I've wanted nothing from you except that you believe me." Before the question came, he felt gnawing at his mind the thought that she must have had other men since they parted. He wanted to cry out to her to keep quiet or to run out, but she continued, "Why did you take the role?"

The quiet calm with which he replied in its perfunctoriness fell just short of flippancy. "Oh, many reasons. I'm an actor. And, after all, it's a good role." They both giggled at his exaggerated grand gesture as he extended his arm in a sweep and returned it to rest on his breast, "Myself."

He was much encouraged by her laughter. "If the play goes and Davis keeps his promise, it'll mean some kind of run in New York." His voice trailed off tentatively for he wanted to add, " . . . for both of us."

But Valerie quickly came in. "I can't believe that is your reason, really your reason. I feel that this vulgar exhibition of our lives is cheap, and degrading. I had hoped our ugly story would be forgotten." She continued her expression of her revulsion by quoting Vergil Davis. He had insisted that the public's insatiable curiosity would never let them find peace in oblivion. The proscenium would become one gigantic peephole into their souls. "I think I've always been stronger than you, Scotty. I've tried to think of this as just another role, one I needed desperately. But not you, Scotty. You took it for another reason. An actor and a good role? You're not the type. That's not your real reason."

This was his chance—whether he ever admitted it to himself or not—the moment he had hoped for these past few agonizing years of being without her. If he were a writer, this would be the cue in the dialogue to tell her simply and honestly that he wanted to be near her again. But some perversity, some compulsive intellectualization, impelled him to say, "Perhaps not. Call it public psychoanalysis. I've thought about us often, almost all the time, constantly." Perhaps he should not have said that; it sounded as though he were begging. He continued, "I've constantly thought about the shooting, the trial, about you, especially about you." There, he said it—and she didn't say a word.

He rose and walked toward the door and breathed in as though he could never get enough of the air. Then he turned back to her. "The more I thought, the more I sank back into my emotional, irrational cell from which I couldn't break out so that I might see things objectively, intellectually. When Vergil offered me the role, I grabbed it. I figured that in reliving our lives in this play I might be able to see things more objectively, analyze my role as I usually do a part I have in any play I'm in. That way I might find a clue, an understanding of other characters, their relationship to me and I to them, especially to you. Remember how we used to analyze the roles we played, the way we used to reconstruct the complete biographies of the characters we played, their entire lives, even though in a play we only played a brief moment in their lives.?"

Yes, she did recall. Oh God, how much she recalled! They took their art so seriously. Even when they were in plays that ran for month after month, each performance was like opening night. And yes, she told him, that was precisely the point. She, too, hoped to look at her part as a role in a play, place herself under the microscope, and observe her reaction to all other characters, yes, even to him. Then she might be able to free herself from the tormenting self-pity, from her self-righteousness, her self-dramatization ...

If only he had the courage to rush to her, to take her in his arms, to comfort her, and to tell her how they needed each other. But he told her how he, too, felt that way; he particularly wondered about his self-righteousness and how it was so contrary to his image of himself as a modern man.

"Soooo," she taunted him, "You've begun to doubt your 'role' in the 'scandal.'"

Her sneer deflated him. He protested to her that he had honestly tried to understand, at that very horrible time in their lives. When she attacked him for his arrogance, for having arrogated to himself the only available cloak of honesty that he would not share with another, for having claimed a monopoly on honesty, he feebly offered that perhaps he was not the "modern" man he had thought himself to be.

"Just an old-fashioned boy ...," she started to say and then laughed in her all-knowing way. "What's happening, Scotty? Look, we're starting to quarrel. And only about words. I don't want to quarrel with you. Let's get back into character. We're actors, and this is another job, and that's all."

Her laughter gave him the courage to ask, "Then why did you break down the first day of rehearsal?"

She turned away from him, with a wave of her hand as though to ward off a blow. "That's over and done with. Please change the subject."

When Scotty insisted she answer, she slowly tried to explain. It was all simple. The human being asserted itself above the actress. Her emotions took control. There once was a part of her life that meant everything to her. How does one tear it out and discard it? Does one awake one morning and proclaim she has become a new, a different person? How easy, isn't it?

Simply shed one's life like a snake its skin?
Her painful groping for an explanation distressed him. He was about to step toward her when she again laughed. "It's 'method' acting, don't you see? I was immersing myself in the role, living the part. No, really, that's nonsense. I saw you again, I saw Sinclair again, face-to-face with both of you for the first time since the trial . . . so I indulged in a wee bit of humanness, that's all. I . . . I . . . oh, it's too simple, and if you don't understand . . ."

He assured her that he did understand. They moodily returned to silence. He could not concentrate. Soon he ventured, "Will you have dinner with me? Tonight?"

"No."

He controlled himself and did not yield to the impulse to ask why, to press the point. Yet, he wondered why. She must have understood his bafflement, and she did want to tell him. She rested her script on her lap as she spoke.

"If you only knew how I've wanted you to ask me. How I've hoped each time the phone rang that it was your voice saying hello . . . No, I'm sorry, Scotty. Dinner is out. Davis got me to promise not to. He doesn't want us to be seen in public together. His publicity is building up some nonsense that we are bitter enemies, and this production is like some sort of grudge fight."

They both agreed that it was all infantile nonsense. He had doubts at that moment whether he had been wise to accept the role. There had been times when his interpretation of a role ran counter to that of the director; then he had to submerge, in addition to obliterating his own personality, his own conception. At those times he felt himself completely emasculated. Now, the horror—his own, very real life, was a piece of theatrical property to be manipulated and promoted by others.

He wanted to ask Valerie whether she, too, had second thoughts, had . . . Oh, what's the use, he decided. Dear, brave, beloved Valerie had been through enough of an ordeal.

Why should he plague her with another barrage of questions? Enough. Ah yes, it was enough for him to handle his interminable nightmares when he'd awake to the shot of the gun. Would he break down, too, like Valerie had when the scene will come when he will again be aiming a gun at Sinclair? Yes, it will be a blank bullet, and nothing will happen except that Sinclair will act his part, pretend he'd been wounded ... Will that purge him of the horror? While memorizing his lines, when he had come to that scene, he became almost paralyzed, without a will—as though the gun was the brain directing him to press the trigger.

What if he had really killed Sinclair? Yes, that's it! He was horrified to think that he still, unconsciously, wanted to finish the job, to kill ...

Valerie looked up at him in puzzlement at his sudden, quiet laughter. Before he could explain his bête noire Sinclair Turner entered. Scotty turned to her and quietly said, "I'll be glad when it's over."

She smiled, "That's my cue in a play in which I came in with, 'And so we wish our precious lives away.'"

"Good morning." Sinclair's greeting was accompanied by a tentative and pleadingly conciliatory smile. When the two remained turned away from him in silence, he tried again. "Oh, come. We're grown-up, mature people. After all, I was the one who was shot. I'm willing to forget the past. We can't keep living in the past. Time and people change ..."

Valerie spoke to Everett. "I think I'll sit in the sun till the call."

As Scotty followed her, he invitingly suggested that he'd be walking by the river after dinner. She smiled. They stopped briefly at the door to exchange greetings with a breathless Ellen.

10
Ingenue and Juvenile

The only one Ellen saw when coming onstage was a morose Sinclair.

"I thought I was late. Isn't anyone else here?"

"You just passed our two stars."

"We have three stars. You, Sinclair ... "

"Thank you. I'll be glad when these two weeks are over. I didn't expect that Everett would still be obsessed with his jealous monomania, his hatred."

"Oh, I'm sorry you feel that way. I thought you were going to be in the Broadway production."

"What Broadway production? Who's going to produce it?"

"But Mr. Davis said ... "

"Mr. Davis says a lot—too much! You'll learn, my dear Ellen, that in this business you can't believe anyone. The only time you can believe is when you actually see the curtain going up. Even, then, when it goes down on opening night, that might be the play's last." To her openmouthed puzzlement he continued, "The critics, you know."

"Oh."

"Oh, what the hell. It's a lovely morning, you're so fresh and beautiful, and so filled with illusions, hope, optimism . . . ."

And she was truly all that and more. Who could blame the jaded, bitter actor for reaching out for some contact with elusive youth? He desperately needed her warm acceptance at that moment. For that one moment his bravado had crumpled and he had pitied himself. She felt drawn to this man, this man who needed her. She took a step toward him ...

At that moment a disheveled, ghastly looking Joseph came in and stood staring at her. He walked with a grin toward Sinclair, and then whirled around to her again. Her attempt to smile at him was quickly aborted by the contemptuous look on his face.

"I think I'll take some sun till the call." She turned toward the door.

Joseph snapped back, "Can you recognize the call when you hear it?"

"What do you mean?"

"There are all kinds of calls—and callings—and call girls ..."

Before she could reach him to slap his face, Sinclair stepped between them.

She spluttered out, "You degenerate little beast ..."

"I'll handle him," Sinclair grimly nodded to her. She controlled her tears as she furiously rushed out. Sinclair walked a few steps after her, for he intended to reassure or console her. He stopped and turned back when he heard Joseph's taunt.

"Getting yourself pretty cosy with that little bitch ...."

"Where have you been?"

"I've been ... wouldn't you like to know! Worried about your meal ticket, eh?"

Sinclair might have guessed where Joseph had been. He had heard that Joseph had last been seen at one of the bars in the next town and had left with a young girl and an older man close to midnight the night before last. The girl was a newcomer to the town, but the man was well known. He drove a Buick station wagon and made frequent trips in it to Boston and New York. No one knew what business he was in, but speculation linked him with a variety of bizarre activities, from gambling to drugs. No one really knew. But Sinclair would have been wrong in his guess, and as circumstances developed, Sinclair would never know.

Less than a week later, everyone in the company, in the town, in the world, would learn that Joseph had spent that past day and a night in a jail just over the state line. A few phone calls to and from his famous father in Hollywood got him out on bail and kept the incident from the press, but his two companions were still there when he left.

Sinclair stood silently brooding. He then sat down and opened his script. He gave no response when Joseph screamed at him, "Well?" The young man ran uncertainly toward the exit, then back again toward the stair to the dressing rooms, stopped and turned on Sinclair.

"Silent treatment, huh? Think you're like my old man. Close me up in my room without supper. What do you think I am? I'm not going to wait around while you chase every little chippy in skirts . . ."

Quietly and deliberately, Sinclair put down his script, rose and closed in on Joseph. "I think I know what you need . . ." Quickly he landed a powerful slap on the other's face.

Joseph cringed and whimpered, "Don't, don't . . ."

"Where have you been? You haven't been in your room for two nights. I heard about you the night before last, playing the big shot down at the Blue Goose, standing everyone to a round of drinks, again and again. Where'd you get the money? You borrowed five bucks from me, said you were broke."

Failing to get an answer, Sinclair grabbed him at the throat and raised his hand to strike again, "Answer me!"

"Davis gave me an advance."

"Why weren't you at rehearsal yesterday? Where were you"

"I don't know."

Sinclair again raised his threatening hand, "What do you mean, you don't know? Out with it. You can piss away your career, but you're not going to make a fool out of me . . ."

Amidst a clatter of noise, Marilyn and Dr. Strong, carrying

a fireplace between them, quickly came through the door. They were followed by Dobrow and Bobby who carried two stage flats between them. Quickly, Sinclair disengaged himself from Joseph and tried to simulate nonchalance as he walked away from the others and pretended to be absorbed in his script. With efficient authority Sam Dobrow directed the others where to set up the flats and fit the fireplace into position. With a simper of, "Don't you think I ought to know," Bobby ignored him and went about the business of supervising the work. Dobrow shrugged his shoulders and turned toward Joseph. He looked inquiringly at the youth who slumped away from him into a chair.

All the stage manager offered was, "Soooo, you're back . . . "

Dr. Strong stepped away from the set and turned to Sinclair. "Good morning, Mr. Turner." Sinclair's affable response was a credit to his acting ability, for he was most gracious, was a picture of a man completely at peace with the world.

The doctor saw Joseph. "Hello, Joseph. Sayyyyy, you don't look so good. Let me feel your pulse." Strong approached Joseph who jumped up with an "I'm fine. I'm O.K." and bolted off stage and down to his dressing room.

The others and the doctor first looked at each other with raised eyebrows and mystification, then they turned inquiringly toward the older actor. At first he tried to shrug them off with a helpless gesture of resignation, of a suggestion of "what do you expect me to say"; but they stood staring at him. He turned away with, "He'll be O.K. Just needs some sleep and food."

Of course, much to Dobrow's disgust, Marilyn would come in with her brash wisdom, "Everyone is deluded into thinking that all a person requires is to satisfy the tissue needs . . . ."

Apparently the young apprentice amused Dr. Strong who asked her, "And what do you need beyond your tissue needs?"

The other impatiently waved down his intensity. "Actors are actors, and they'll act if they have to kill their mothers for a role. The amenities between decent people have nothing to do with actors. When it comes to loyalties, forget about these mummers ..."

Was the producer taunting him? No one knew better than Marc the kernel of truth in Davis's contemptuous assertion. It was at the very bottom of his own despairing situation, for he had been vilely victimized, been betrayed, been practically destroyed by ... whom? He was confidently certain that it was an actor who had been the turncoat who had rejected and turned against all their ideals, their united front, and their affirmations during the war against Fascism. He suspected who had spoken the words that had barred him from the film lots in Hollywood during the hysteria of the cold-war inquisitorial years. He wanted to refute the producer's blanket, destructive dismissal of common decency and humanity from actors. But what could he say with conviction? Davis knew that he had succeeded in silencing his director and continued by using an assumed dialect of his notion of a Viennese psychiatrist in order to relieve Marc's tenseness.

"Soooo, Valerie is having her hysterics. It was inevitable and fits the pattern of her syndrome. Better she have it now than on opening night, no? She'll get this out of her system, and she'll be the good professional that she is from now on."

The glum look on his companion's face obliged Davis to resume his own voice.

"C'mon, Marc, let's get on with it and concentrate on the set. Have you given your O.K.? I've got a list of lumber, paint, canvass, and God knows what else from Bobby for ten seasons at the Metropolitan Opera."

"It's not such a simple set. Sinclair's living room has to reveal his Bohemian sophistication. Whatever else anyone may think of Bobby, he knows his business. He's a genius with this multiple unit set. Just look at how he worked out the scrim effect ..."

Vergil Davis impatiently assumed the vulgar voice of Marlon Brando as Stanley Kowalski, "Don' gimme any of dese artsy productions. Dis is a straight mellerdrama. Jes keep it dat way 'n leave d' artsy-fartsy stuff to da collitches 'n Greenwitch Village. Jes don' ferget we're jes' simple Americans."

The woebegone look on Marc's face softened Davis's crassness and insensitive arrogance. It wasn't only that he couldn't do without Marc at this point; he also had a long-standing and deep-rooted affection and respect for him. He placed his arm around Marc's shoulder and assured him that it will all work out, that the temperamental actors will come around and be the docile troupers they were supposed to be. He followed his spiel with an attempt to build Marc's ego.

"I accepted the play exactly the way you wrote it. I have faith in you, and I respect the faith you have in your characters as real people. I guess I've been around actors too long. I see them as commodities, two for a nickel, and that's how I know them—with a few, yes very few, exceptions. Oh, I know, Valerie is one of those exceptions."

The director-author would not let it rest at that. "You think you know them. You could be wrong, you know. People are people. These poor slobs go from job to job—that is, if they have a job to go to. How can they feel secure and behave like any other Joe with a nine-to-five job? I suppose that's what helps them immerse themselves in a role, they try to find some kind of identity in the characters they play, to live vicariously . . ."

"Okay, okay. So all right already." With all the urgencies of being a producer pressing on him, Vergil Davis was not inclined to get into a sociological discussion with his director. In spite of himself, he was sucked into pursuing the discussion because of his strong feelings on the subject as well as his respect and admiration for Marc. He tried to have the last word and shut off this fruitless debate.

"So, who forced them to be actors? Anyway, I'm glad you feel the way you do. That's as it should be. And you direct them with the conviction you have about them, and we'll have a good—no, a great play. But I want you to know that I've yet to find an actor who won't kiss the producers' royal asses before he gets his contract. Then, once he's got his contract, the producer can't even talk to him. As long as I've got to deal with actors, I'll stick to my opinion." With derision, he added, "Finding their identity—ugh, balls I say!"

"I'm like them, in spades, Vergil. You know damn well I'm trying to find my identity too."

"Cool it. What's all this melodrama about? Now don't you get impatient. I made a promise and I'll keep it. When we sell this play to the movies, everything will be just fine. I've got some hot nibbles now, but I can't tell you about them. I've been through this too often. When I've cashed the check, only then I'll be sure. You know as well as I do that you can't count on anything in this stupid business—even after the curtain goes up."

This sounded all-too-familiar to Marc, who waved aside Davis's chatter. He tapped his jacket to indicate his inside pocket, "I got a letter . . ."

Quickly, and almost too cautiously, Davis asked, "From whom?"

"From my son. When I answer him, how can I tell him that I'm too much of a coward to say that I wrote this play. He's hoping that with this play I'll be established again, his mother and I will get together again, and we'll be one happy family once more."

"Come on, Marc, knock it off. I've done a lot for you and I expect you to live up to your promise. After all, the idea of the play was mine. I let you copyright it as being completely yours."

"But I wrote it—every last word, dot, and exclamation point . . ."

Marc wanted to continue, but suddenly a delayed reaction struck him. Why was Vergil so interested in the letter from his son? Why had he so quickly asked, "From whom?" Should he tell Vergil about the other letter? Vergil might know something about it, and if not he should know. But the producer's absorption in their discussion, despite the fact that he was torn by so many problems, gave Marc pause. He debated with himself whether or not to tell Vergil. Vergil also debated with himself.

How easy it would be to snap back at Marc by telling him that he could have gotten another writer, not just a hack but a good one, with the assurance of at least a summer-stock production. However, he reflected that his long association with Marc must not be disturbed, and he did need him now. Therefore, he continued his original fatherly, indulgent tone and assured Marc of his respect and belief in the writer-director that convinced him that Marc must have this chance, and that is why he guaranteed him a production before he put one sheet into his typewriter. Then, as a warning, he cautioned Marc to have faith in him. Right now Marc's name is mud, the play would never have a film sale if it were known that Marc was the author—while he was on the blacklist, at any rate. In an attempt to change the subject and to put Marc on the defensive, he added, "I still can't understand why you did it. You could have said a few innocuous things, played dumb, kidded them along. Others did it, bigger men than you . . ."

The other was about to explode; instead he quietly, sarcastically observed, "Yes, they are big men, really big, big men. . . ." His sarcasm should have shut off further discussion except from the pragmatic Davis.

"You could have done the same. Look where they are. They're writing under sixteen different names and making plenty of money. Not one of them has your talent. As big as they were in Hollywood, they're getting bigger in TV. I don't know what in hell you're trying to prove."

Wearily, Marc walked away from him. "So, I could be big in TV. And how big would my son think I am if I told him I had weaseled? Let it go. I have faith in you, you have faith in

"I think I'm ready for it—sex."

Although Dr. Strong considered himself more sophisticated than the people of the town and had been exposed to many raw facts of life, he was sufficiently tied to his puritanical background to be embarrassed by the girl's precociousness. He was grateful for Dobrow's matter-of-fact if not gruff pragmatic response, which allowed him to withdraw from further talk on the subject with Marilyn who seemed eager to pursue the subject.

"When do you start? I wish you'd get it over with so that you can concentrate on your work." With this the stage manager directed her to assist Bobby Francis. The irrepressible Marilyn continued her prattle as she worked.

"I promised my mother I wouldn't. But I specifically told her that the promise is for this summer only. I have plans to do considerable research on the subject when I start college in the fall."

Having pushed the fireplace into its chalked place, Bobby and Dobrow hopped off the apron into the house to determine how it suited. The doctor walked to the wings in order not to obstruct their view and found himself alone with Sinclair.

"Did you notice his eyes?"

With a look of unimpeachable innocence, Sinclair asked, "Whose?"

"Joseph's. They were so glazed. There's something wrong there . . ."

They were interrupted by a call from the stage manager, "Dr. Strong, and Mr. Turner, please just walk across the stage and then stand for a moment anywhere on the set. We want to see how the fireplace and the flats work with the action."

The two men obliged. Dobrow thanked them and turned to discuss the set with the designer. Dr. Strong thought that Sinclair's deliberate turning away from him at that point, no matter how casual the actor seemed to make the movement, was a deliberate attempt to avoid discussing Joseph. The doctor was determined to follow through and again approached

Sinclair when he heard himself hailed from the door. It was the trooper.

"How're you doing, Doc?"

"Oh, hello, Wally. You're not looking for me, are you? No emergencies, are there?"

"No. You just enjoy your vacation. I'm looking for Mr. Dobrow. Is he around?"

The voice of the stage manager called him from the darkened auditorium, "I'm down here." Dobrow hurried down the aisle and quickly jumped up onto the stage. "What can I do for you?"

"I've got good news for you on the gun permit, Mr. Dobrow. As long as it's a stage prop your permit covers you and the entire show. It's to be handled only by the actors indicated in the script. You're responsible for it, so you've got to take care of it when it's not in use on the stage. If anyone gets it, you won't be in dutch, but if it's found in anyone's possession off stage, that person gets into trouble."

"That's fine. I'll take care of it. I appreciate your trouble."

"Anytime. Glad to help."

Dobrow took the permit, scanned it, and then placed it in his wallet.

Marilyn gushingly engaged Wally in conversation; for this the doctor was grateful, for he wanted his intended conversation with the trooper to come about casually.

"Remember your promise to your mother, Marilyn," and to Wally's puzzled expression, the doctor offered, "Just a private joke, Wally."

Dobrow called Marilyn back to her work, and Dr. Strong and the trooper strolled outdoors toward the prowl car. Certain that no one could hear them, Wally asked the doctor if he'd learned anything new about the drugs that were missing from his bag.

"No, nothing definite. But I've a good idea who the culprit is."

"Want me to move in?"

Ingenue and Juvenile

"The problem is that it could be either Joseph G. Heywood, Jr. or Sinclair Turner. I haven't been able to get into their dressing rooms yet . . ."

"That's easy. I can get the selectmen to ask you to make a routine inspection. They could figure out an excuse and . . ."

"No, Wally. We don't want any rumours started about the company. After all, we want the theater here, and we want them to be successful. Let's keep this problem between just the two of us. I'm confident we'll straighten it out . . . Meanwhile, keep your eye on that young actor while he's around town, and I hear he's around plenty. The older man seems to keep pretty much to himself."

"I don't have to keep my eye on young Joseph Jr.—he's in everyone's eye in town. He got very high the other night across the river. Made a helluva row. I locked him up for his own good. Got him to sleep it off. The next thing I knew they locked him up over the state line, him and a couple of other birds. His old man got him out through a lawyer from Boston, but the other two are still in custody until their records are checked out. They're being held on a drug charge."

The doctor sighed. "I thought our part of the world was safe from that plague."

"You know, doc, that kid isn't really a bad sort. I had a long talk with him. But I can't figure out what he's got against his old man. It would break his heart if he knew what the boy said about him. He wasn't fresh or rough until his old man was mentioned . . ."

The doctor started to giggle. When the trooper looked at him with puzzlement, he said, "We must never let Marilyn know about his antipathy for his father. Gosh, she'd have a field day spouting Freud and the Oedipus complex. But let's get back to my missing drugs. You're sure it wasn't in your car?"

"I pulled it apart, under the seats and everything. And that bag was closed and not out of my sight until I left it for you with the stage manager. Say, do you suppose he . . . ?"

"I can't answer for anyone when it comes to drugs. But if I'm any judge of human nature, I'd be willing to swear he had nothing to do with the theft. I'll have to stir my rump about it though. There was enough there to kill an elephant if someone who doesn't know takes only a tenth of it. I still think we should broadcast a warning."

"I've taken this up with my chief and we both agreed. The stuff was not lost; it was stolen. We're sure of that. Whoever stole it knows pretty darn well what it is, so we're not worried about an overdose. You said there was enough for at least a month's supply for a heavy user. Well, give us a couple more days."

They both saw Marc Denis hurrying toward them on his way to the stage entrance. The trooper greeted Marc, got into his car, and drove off while Marc and Dcotor Strong went into the theater.

11

Places, Please!

"Let's go, everybody. We start with twenty-one."

The quiet vigor of Marc's voice as he announced, in the language of the theater, that the rehearsal would start with act 2, scene 1, infected the others with enthusiasm despite its authoritativeness. That is, to all but his stage manager.

"One moment, Marc. I've got to check a few items with you." Sam moved determinedly down stage left on the apron and away from the others so that he could speak privately with Marc. While coming down to meet Sam, Marc hailed Bobby Francis.

"I want to check a few items with you, Bobby."

"Yes?"

"Get your sky piece and scrim up as soon as you can. When?"

"And where am I supposed to get canvas, pulleys, lumber, cord, and God knows what else?"

"See Mr. Davis. Hold it. You mean to say you haven't started on them yet? What in hell goes on here!"

Bobby became almost hysterical. "It's not my fault if I don't get help—no apprentices, no material, no . . ."

This all gave Marc a feeling of déjà vu. These problems were par for the course, and so he remained unruffled. He calmly turned to Bobby and spoke quietly but with a firmness that foreclosed any rebuttals.

"It's your responsibility. I want it up first thing in the morning even if it means your staying with it all night."

Bobby started to sputter a protest, which Marc quickly cut off.

"If you have any gripes, see Davis. And furthermore, I don't like the colors you've planned."

"But the lighting . . ."

"I've used gels over my flashlight to light your model. It won't do. Period! After dinner, we meet here tonight. Be here at 7:30. Sam, you be here, too. I'll give you the working light plot by then. Now, Sam, what's on your mind?"

The stage manager grinned and waved toward Bobby. "He's covered it."

Sulking and grumbling, Bobby fussed around the set. Marc returned Sam's grin.

"O.K., Sam, call it. Top of twenty-one."

The others tensed while Sam took his place at his table on the stage apron.

"Places! Top of twenty-one, everybody. Clear the stage."

Bobby whirled to glower at Sam, gathered his paraphernalia, and retreated with what dignity he could muster.

Sam raised his hand to signal the start when Marc interrupted.

"Hold it. Where's Joseph?"

The silence that followed was relieved when Sinclair volunteered, "I'll get him."

Sinclair hurried down the stairs before Marc could stop him. As a director, Marc didn't want any actor doing errands, and he wanted to intercept Sinclair, but it was too late. Everett rose and spoke with resolution.

"If I had my way, I'd eliminate his role."

It was apparent that Everett had not spoken purely from an emotional disgust evoked by Joseph's unprofessional behavior. The silence that greeted his statement revealed bewilderment, doubt, and could undermine the cast. Marc knew that the actors must have faith, childlike though it may be, in the play in order that they play their roles with conviction. Had anyone else, say Davis, brought up this doubt in the validity of the role, Marc would have demolished the suggestion with a cold, curt assertion that the creative art was his province. But Everett could not be so dismissed. After all, he was the real-life principal in this play. Yet, Marc *knew* that his own concept, his own development of the play was absolutely right. But suppose Everett had some insight that eluded Marc, had some . . . Marc's struggle within himself of how to meet this challenge was cut short when Valerie roused herself.

"But you can't eliminate him. My brother was important to me. Important to the things that happened."

As though he were far away in that time past, Everett repeated, "We should eliminate him."

Ah, this was exciting, thought Marc. He quietly turned to Everett and spoke with respect. "This is important, Scotty. Now, you say we should eliminate the role, and Valerie not only disagrees but she emphasizes that the role is important. Tell us, why did you say we should eliminate the role?"

"I don't know. It just came out. I wasn't thinking."

"Precisely. You weren't thinking. But you were feeling, and that's more important. You weren't aware of it. Now, for the first time, unless I'm mistaken, you've expressed your unconscious thoughts. You've always resented Valerie's brother. You've resented anyone for whom she had affection . . ."

Everett's denial was hot and passionate. "Not her brother. I liked the kid. I was sick, I wept like a baby when he was lost in Korea."

"I'm not a psychiatrist, but I'd bet you wept because of your guilt—of which you weren't aware then, and still aren't aware. When you said we should eliminate the role, you were expressing your unconscious desire to eliminate all traces of his memory, the symbol of your guilt feelings."

"But I liked him . . . he was a good kid. . . ." Everett desperately tried to subdue his apparent anguish. "He put up with a lot from me. . . ."

"De nihil nisi bonum. Speak only well of the dead. God knows, Scotty, basically you've got good instincts. Maybe, when you got news of his death, you compensated for your resentment of him by a very human sentimental response. That sounds better than guilt feelings. You were the actor responding on cue."

Now he strongly shot back at Marc, "Not as an actor! As a simple human being. An actor has his own life, too, off stage, in life, between him and other day-to-day human beings . . ."

"We shall see. That's your challenge in this role. . . ."

The entrance of Sinclair, followed by Joseph, interrupted Marc. Joseph mumbled his apologies. To his "Sorry I'm late, Sir," Marc said, with a businesslike finality that succeeded in covering his anger, "We'll discuss this later. We're late enough as it is. See me at the break. O.K., Sam, let her ride."

Again Sam called, "Places. Top of twenty-one. That's you, Joseph."

What a far cry, thought Dr. Strong, as he watched the others intently concentrating on the rehearsal as though nothing else in the world mattered, from the urgencies of life. Back at the hospital his patients were in various torments of lingering death. Should he not be there, with them, instead of with these overgrown children who, if challenged, would equate their dedication to make-believe with his work of easing pain? In his eighteen years of medical practice he had been almost daily drawn into conflicts with his conscience whether or not to leave the bedside of one in agony so that he could merely cater to his own urgent needs of food or sleep. He welcomed this respite so that he could come back to his work with more professional objectivity.

His unusually large supply of drugs that had been pilfered from him was not the small emergency dosage he normally carried with him. Perhaps some justice was being visited upon him for his entertaining the thought of easing old man Perkins out of his misery. The Perkins family had been close to his. He had grown up with the Perkins children. The old man had been the doctor's closest friend. Doc Strong had no right to hasten the inevitable end, yet he prayed the old man would die quickly—he prayed that *all* cancer victims could quickly die. The doctor resented the illogical strength of the old man's heart. An insulin shock could finish him off, but the nurse would know. The drugs would do it . . . but they were gone. Oh yes, he could easily get another supply. Yet he hesitated: was he being given a warning by a mysterious providence through the disappearance of the drug? He tormented himself by sneering at his unscientific superstition. He forced himself to concentrate on the rehearsal.

Valerie had seated herself, script in hand, but she rarely referred to it, for she was a "quick study" and learned her lines with the aid of an uncanny photographic memory. Joseph, script in hand, entered. Valerie jumped up from the sofa and eagerly questioned him.

"*Have you found him?*"

"*No.*"

"*What shall I do?*"

Joseph read from his script, "*What happened last night?*"

"*It's been two nights. And I told you what happened. He simply refused to believe that you were with me at Sinclair Turner's for lunch. I don't know how to handle him, no less what to say to him any more. Outside of radio he hasn't had a decent role in over a year. If that's hell for anyone, it's ten hells for an actor. He's got to keep up appearances for everyone, and then when he gets home the stress of the tension breaks him all up. He'll say or do anything, and I know he doesn't mean it.*"

She stopped and indecisively sat on the edge of the sofa while Joseph mechanically turned from her and toyed with the top of a chair. Then she continued.

"*I think he's jealous of my job. He resents it while he's sitting around offices just waiting. God, I know how it feels. I think a slave market is paradise compared to that waiting and waiting, that coming back again and again, that effort to* smile, to look one's best. At least the slave knows his fate all at once. To sit there with other actors and then to be interviewed and read for a part only to have the actor with whom you've been friendly five minutes before walk off with the part, and then you hate that actor but smile and wish him luck. Ugh!"

Joseph read from the script, "*I don't think that's the reason. He just doesn't like me, doesn't like Sinclair, doesn't like anyone . . .*"

Marc interrupted him with a bark, "Hold it. What's with the script in your hand, Joseph?"

"I'm sorry, Sir. Till I get the feel of it, I find it helps me realize the role better. Once I feel I'm living the role, I'll discard the script."

A groan came from Sam, "Oh my God—the 'method' rides again."

Impatiently, Marc squelched Sam. "Quiet, Sam. Now, Joseph, that may be O.K. anyplace else. But this is summer stock. We've no time for your individual approach. This isn't Broadway with four weeks of rehearsal. Five, six days at most, and the play goes on, line-perfect. We won't stop now, but starting with your next scene, no script in sight."

A most humble Joseph whispered "Yes Sir."

"Once again, start from the top of twenty-one."

Marc impatiently lit a cigarette while Joseph left the stage to place himself for his entrance and Valerie rearranged herself on the sofa. Dobrow repeated his call for places when Marc interrupted.

"No. We've no time to go back. Take it with Joseph's speech that I interrupted."

They resumed, with Joseph reading his role.

"*I don't think that's the reason. He just doesn't like me, doesn't like Sinclair, doesn't like anyone . . . I don't think he even likes himself.*"

Her voice now carried a deeper emotion than required for a rehearsal, "*That's the most terrible part of it. That's why he must never doubt that I love him.*"

Places, Please!

Everett entered. He hesitated a moment and then with the trace of a sneer raised his arms in mock benediction, "*Blessings on this happy home.*"

Valerie rose and with an eager smile greeted him, "*Hello, darling.*"

Joseph echoed her, "*Hello, Scotty.*"

Valerie continued, "*I was worried about you . . .*"

"*And who comforted you? Your brave big brother? Or did you find the broad shoulders of another, say like . . .*"

Valerie raised her hand to stop him when Joseph spoke, "*What's this new role, Scotty? You rehearsing for Othello or something?*"

"*My dear, sweet brother-in-law, your mature understanding of people, your codification of human emotions, your possibly sincere and at other times gratifying interest in my professional roles, your natal ties with my wife manifest in your constant attendance upon her, your clean-living American idealism demonstrated by your interset in and defense of your sister's welfare, in her ill-advised alliance with a down-and-out no talent hambo, all do you justice, do justice to the society that spawned you. But keep your snotty nose out of my affairs! Get out of here and stay the hell out!*"

Joseph stood uncertainly looking at Valerie. She quickly urged him, "*Do go, Joseph. Everything will be all right.*"

At first he was undecided, and then Joseph reluctantly turned to go. Valerie accompanied him to the door where he turned to her, "*Goodbye, dear.*"

"*I'll phone you tomorrow,*" she promised him as she closed the door behind him.

Everett crushed his script in both hands as he suddenly walked out of the scene and down toward Marc.

"Hold it, Marc. It couldn't have been that way. I know I was harsh with him. There isn't a moment since that I haven't been sorry. But, God, man, that was the last time I saw him or spoke with him while he was alive. I couldn't have called him names . . . Marc, the kid's dead . . ."

With a sigh of resignation, Marc announced, "Take five minutes, everybody."

He grumbled to Sam, "This isn't a rehearsal of a play. It's a psychiatric clinic. I'm beginning to think I'm one of the patients. I'm sure as hell not one of the doctors."

Perhaps Valerie could extricate them out of this new roadblock. Marc nodded encouragement to Valerie who took Everett aside and engaged him in a discussion about what was, presumably, his dilemma. Bobby loitered near the stage door, nodded to Marilyn, and then left again.

12

The Actors Prepare

Marc impatiently pretended to discuss technical details with his stage manager while furtively watching Valerie and Everett. With much relief Marc noted the nodding of Everett's head in response to Valerie's earnest, quiet talk. Quickly, a subdued and calm Everett turned to Marc.

"I'm sorry, Marc. Let's get on with it. I promise to behave."

"From where?" Dobrow turned to Marc for instructions.

"Right on—from Joseph's exit."

Dobrow, who had been shaking his head despairingly, roused himself and barked out with businesslike authority, "Places. Twenty-one, middle of page five, after Joe's exit."

The scene continued, and Marc was confident that it would run smoothly in the hands of the professionals. Too bad, he thought, that Valerie's personal life had interfered with a gloriously promising career. How deliciously sophisticated she had been when he saw her in a road company of Molnár's *The Guardsman* and in a West Coast production of the same author's *The Play's the Thing*. So sophisticated, so witty, as though the famous Hungarian had written the roles with her in mind. And here was the scintillating star playing in her own tragedy. Alas, he thought, that this great talent had been arrested at the very moment it was to achieve the actress's ambition. Oh well, perhaps this play may launch her into orbit once more. Alert to the action, Marc stood poised, with pencil in one hand and clipboard in the other, to jot down his notes with which he would compliment or correct the actors after the rehearsal. The scene continued with Valerie once again in character:

"Joe has been a great comfort to me these past couple of days while you were . . . gone."

Everett came in on cue, "O.K., O.K. Soooo, sweet, cute little brother has been a comfort to you. A little incest now and then is relished by the best of men–and women."

"You're depraved, wicked, and monstrous!"

"Not half as much as your other boyfriend. Did he come around to take his turn with his special style of comfort?"

She took a step toward him. "Scotty, please darling . . . you will hate yourself for saying all these things to me. Please don't be so horrible. I haven't stirred out of the house in two days, waiting for you, worrying . . . desperate. I love you darling. Only you. Please believe me, there is no one else but you."

He stood confused as she embraced him. He raised his face to her, looked deeply into her eyes, started to say something, then buried his face with a sigh into her bosom. His muffled voice said, "I don't know—I don't—know . . ."

"Say that you believe me. You know I love only you. There never can be anyone else. No one but you . . . forever . . ."

They clung to one another. She kissed him and said, "Go tidy up. I'll get dinner ready."

"Yes, make dinner. You've made and paid for so many, one more won't matter."

"You big baby . . ."

He unbent slightly and exited right. Valerie busied herself with imaginary props in setting a table. The stage manager simulated the ring of a bell, "Brnng." Valerie crossed to the door, opened it to discover Sinclair Turner there. He entered and held forth flowers. Valerie was the first to speak.

"Oh, my God!"

"Thanks, but it's only a very mortal I."

"I'm sorry . . . I wasn't expecting . . . Hello."

Casually and affably, taking advantage of her confusion, Sinclair came into the room. His voice indicated nothing but sincere concern.

"Your absence from rehearsal these past two days worried us ... worried me."

Almost incoherent, Valerie frantically tried to bar his way.

"I'm sorry. I'm sor ... I mean I'm sorry I worried them ... I mean you, everybody. I'm sorry I can't ask you to stay. I'm sorry ... I'm just ... sorry ..."

She was almost in tears. He tried to cheer her.

"Oh, come my dear. Things can't be that bad. Here, I brought you some flowers."

"Oh, no!"

He grandly quoted from Cyrano, "Why so great a no?"

"Please, don't be angry. I'm sorry. But please, you must go. And, please take these ..."

He interrupted her protests by placing his hand on her shoulder.

"You mustn't be so upset. Here, take them. Consider them from the entire company ..."

Everett entered. Valerie eagerly turned to him.

"Scotty, Mr. Turner has come to ask if I'm well enough to come to rehearsal tomorrow."

Everett glared at them. "Why not rehearse right now ... here. I'll clear out. Oh, just don't worry about me."

Valerie was almost hysterical. "Please, Scotty. For God's sake!"

Sinclair turned to go. "Sorry I intruded."

Everett taunted him, "Why not leave the pretty flowers for the lady?"

With this, Everett intercepted Sinclair, grabbed the flowers, tore a card attached to the bouquet from the bunch, and tossed the flowers onto the table. He read the card aloud.

"Missed you. Devotedly, Sinclair."

The pause that followed was broken by Sinclair. "Well?"

"I want to warn you. Stay away from my wife. I know all

about you, you lecherous bastard."

A distraught Valerie projected herself between them.

"Please, Mr. Turner, don't listen. Just go . . . please. I'll be at rehearsal tomorrow."

Before Everett could pick up his line, Sinclair raised his hand. "Hold it." he walked down to Marc.

"Now just a minute. I don't feel right at this point. The next scene in which I appear is just before the shooting scene, the one where I seduce the ingenue . . ."

Demonstrating his disgust with the interruptions, Sam slumped down in his seat. Marc reassured him by patting him on his shoulder and nodded to Sinclair to continue.

"Everett goes out and I'm left alone with Valerie. At this point, right here, there should be something in my lines to vindicate me, to show that I'm not the villain in the piece. There is no honest-to-goodness dirty villain in modern drama. Each character has a psychological motivation. Where is it for me? There must be redeeming elements. The way it's written I leave—out into the night after Everett. That gives the character no dimensions. My next scene with Valerie is where I honestly, sincerely try to help her, and it's misunderstood. It's not clear to the audience. There are no downright villains in modern . . ."

Everett snapped out brutally, "How about Hitler?"

Sinclair, who had tried not to address Everett directly, turned on him, "You miserable crumb . . ."

Before they could tangle with one another, Sam and Marc jumped between them. Over their heads, Sinclair screamed out, "He drove his wife from him by his madness. He's nuts, and he tried to blame me for his own . . ."

"You might be man enough to tell the truth for once . . ."

Despite Marc's efforts to quiet him, Everett continued, "Go on, tell the truth, that you made love to my wife . . ."

Sinclair started to laugh and said, "So, you really want to know."

Valerie shouted at Sinclair, "Don't answer him." Then she

turned on Everett and stood up to him with an accusing arm. "How dare you . . ." She faltered and helplessly walked away as she mumbled, "I suppose another piece of humiliation doesn't matter any more."

Now Everett became contrite and tried to cover it with a bravado. "Come, come. We're all actors. Let's get at the truth so that we can understand our roles, our relationships, with nothing hidden."

But Sinclair would not let it rest. "You can't bluff your way out of it. You're just a jealous wretch. Grow up, will you. You're divorced and have no legal rights. But you cling to your jealousy." He turned to Marc. "Sorry, Marc, I didn't start this. Just to show you, and no one else but you—my director—I will honestly answer the way I did in court—NO! I never made an overt or implied pass at Mrs. Everett Scott."

Why oh why, thought Marc, didn't this man grow up, when Everett snapped back at Sinclair, "You know damn well if you said differently you might come up for perjury."

"If it will help us get through this production with a minimum of friction, I will tell you privately what the truth is. It will be the same—NO! But I'm not talking to you other than that in private or otherwise except as called for in the script."

Desperately, Marc firmly announced, "Let's get on with it. All talk from now on is to be from the script." He nodded to Dobrow.

Seating himself at his table, Dobrow announced, "Places everybody."

While the others took their places, Sinclair stood irresolutely where he was.

"Well, what now?" Marc restrained his impatience and spoke affably.

"You've got to listen to me. This'll take a minute. I know I'm typecast. I played the role in real life and now I'm to enact it on stage. I'm not worried one bit about that. But the lines aren't there. Every character has his roots somewhere in the script, it explains what makes each one tick—every actor, that is, but me. I walk through the play, I give cues, I leer, I'm the heavy, I disrupt a happy marriage, and so on and on. But why do I do these things? The author should give me one scene, one little speech to show how I got so involved, why I supposedly behaved as I did, or at least to show the truth that it was a piling up of circumstantial coincidence."

He found an ally in Ellen who rushed in to say, "He has a good point in that. An actor should know why he acts one way or another . . . ."

Sam turned slowly to face her and sardonically shook his head. His attitude implied to her that he was going to give her a talking to when they were alone again. Her voice faltered while Marc ignored her interruption. His response was directed to Sinclair, but his donnish explanation was intended for all of them.

"I won't buy that. There are theatrical conventions. There is such a thing as recognizable, identifiable evil or the appearance of evil, erroneous as it may be in this character. The author doesn't have to rationalize his character as a product of the slums. This play is a melodrama—no message—no pleas for slum-clearance therapy for a sick society. Judas, Iago, Simon Legree—types. There are good guys and bad guys in a play. That makes the conflict. In this play, you appear as a bad guy only due to circumstances. We hope that the audience will see this because of the richness of the character. I don't want to be arbitrary and close the discussion. But the play, of its kind, satisfies me the way it is written. I'm tired of plays about little guys telling their case histories about broken homes when they were kids, a mother who takes dope, a drunkard father, congenital syphilis, and so on ad nauseum. Shakespeare's 'He hath a lean and hungry look' has stamped the character of Cassius for eternity, and accepted eternally. You have a suave, superb, sophisticated appearance. That is your success or your undoing."

"Don't butter me up. The author avoided answers. Take Everett's role. He would be in his glory among a primitive

The Actors Prepare

tribe where the groom waved the nuptial sheet through the hut's door as proof of the bride's virginity. He makes a fetish of virginity, chastity and all that."

Everett stepped forward, "And lechers like to corrupt the innocent."

The precocious Marilyn saw her opportunity. "If you ask me . . ."

Quickly, Marc shut her up. "Marilyn, please run outside and see if Mr. Davis's car is back."

"I know the answer to the problem. First, take Scotty . . ."

Dobrow shouted at her, "On the double, runt."

"I can teach all of you a few things . . ." Her voice died out when Dobrow rose from his seat. She fled.

Sinclair was still smarting from Everett's assault. "You think you know all the answers, eh? But you're still worried about one question that haunts you."

"This is senseless, Sinclair." Valerie did not look at him. Her voice was wistful. "He knows the answer to that one. If he only had faith. Not in me only, but in himself."

The director and stage manager looked helplessly at one another as Sinclair would not retreat. Marc whispered something to Dobrow to the effect that they may as well, all of them, get it out of their systems.

"It's not that easy. Somewhere in his past he's encountered a shameful episode that drives him to seek all symbols of legitimacy—marriage, home, chastity, the man as the head of the house, and all that jazz. Every word, every line in the script reveals this past that hovers over him. Not so with my part. I don't expect the author to bring in a traumatic episode when a gang of kids on the block dragged me down into the cellar and cockalized me when I was seven years old . . ."

This could go on and on. Yet Marc could not shut him up lest it would undermine Sinclair's rampant confidence. His voice, then, had to indicate respect for Sinclair's analysis and at the same time try to conclude the matter.

"This is summer stock. We have approximately thirty hours

of rehearsal time at most. We cannot call in the author now to rewrite the script. Thank God he isn't in our hair now. This is it! We will do our best, all of us. Any individual problems will be discussed with me privately. Right now we must get on with it. So let's go." Before Dobrow could call the actors to take their places, Sinclair spoke up.

"But the dialogue is so like a sorority bull session at one A.M. It should be over rumpled sheets at high noon—in the nude. This tubercular thing has lung trouble with the fuzz of adolescent romanticism. The characters burst forth into pimples. Let's give them hernias, double hernias, real muscles, real mammaries instead of underendowed tits. This play is about an attempted murder—deep, passionate stuff—I know . . ."

He simply had to cut this short. Marc finally exploded.

"I have faith in this play as it is. Its characters are identifiable without case-history exposition. I also see it as a significant social drama: it shows the dichotomy of the contemporary American idol, a fusion of the glamorized aristocrat of show business and the latent criminal in him. Actors who would like to shoot each other but never have the balls to do it. You represent the romantic, realized lives denied the nine-to-five-two-weeks-vacation-with-pay helots of our society. No more discussion now, and none while we're in rehearsal. See me privately and we'll go into anything you like. On with it, now, from where we left off. If you need a handle, Sinclair, give yourself a limp or a tic. Walk with a limp. Shakespeare used the trick of physical deformity with his King Richard III."

Marc nodded to Sam as he concluded, "No personalities, no interruptions. We shall behave like professionals."

"Places. From the break," announced Sam.

The actors resumed their places. Everett had the first speech.

"*You stay away from my wife. I know all about you, you degenerate bastard.*"

The Actors Prepare

Valerie came in with her speech. *"Please, Mr. Turner, don't listen. Please, just go. I'll be at rehearsal tomorrow."*

Marilyn eagerly came through the stage door; she was followed by Vergil Davis, who was heavily laden with packages. He deposited the packages on Sam's table. One of the packages contained the Noel Coward records, which he held aloft and quietly pointed out to Marc. He stood for a while near Sam and listened to the actors go through their business. During a pause he started to leave. Before doing so he verbally patted Marc on the back with, "They sound good. Looks like one happy family. Keep it up, Marc. We're going to have one helluva great production."

13

The Director's Dilemma

The afterglow of the batik dipped, tumultuous sunset became a deep purple reflection in the slowly flowing Merrimac as it moved by the tree-shaded banks at West Endicott. Marc had sought out this peaceful refuge after his dinner. The past few weeks had entertained a dry spell, so the river was low. The bone-bald rocks above the lazy current appeared ghostlike among the deepening shadows. Turning a bend along the river, he saw two figures a few hundred feet ahead of him. Marc hesitated. On the footpath were Scotty and Valerie. Their slow walk was interrupted when Valerie stumbled. Scotty reached out and grabbed her arm to steady her. After she had righted herself Scotty did not let go, nor did Marc notice that Valerie did anything to disengage his hold. Marc decided to turn back.

Well, he thought, the play may not succeed in the theater, but at least it did succeed in bringing these two together again. Don't be such a priggish do-gooder, he sneered at himself. What in hell will the play do for you! Ah, it must, it will succeed! All his frustrations, all his despair of these past few years of a repressive decade will be brushed aside, buried and forgotten if only.... He had been through worse times. Yes, those Depression years. But then there had been an atmosphere of hope, an affirmative resolve by almost everyone. He mentally shook himself out of the mire of sentimentalizing about those urgent years. He must think of the present. He took stock and was satisfied that he and Vergil had succeeded in keeping his identity, both as the blacklisted director-writer and as the author of the play, hidden from most of the cast and from the local press. Of course, Sinclair and Sam knew who he was. Valerie, Scotty, and Ellen, as well as Joseph, had not known him in the past. If Joseph's father knew who he was in this company, he would most certainly yank his son out of it. The successful one played it safe.

He stopped for a while at a point where a small freshet of a stream busily, illogically rushed noisily into anonymity as it mingled with the indifferent Merrimac. He stood wondering about himself, the dramatist manqué, everlastingly uncertain of his writing. Perhaps it was just as well that he had been blacklisted; it gave him the excuse, the rationale, for not having "made it." He smiled at himself for becoming another Marilyn, the amateur psychoanalyst. But he exulted with the knowledge that as a director he was good! He had confidence in himself, and nothing gave him such ego satisfaction, the sense of fulfillment, the delirious excitement, as he found in directing and then living through his creation after the curtain had risen. Those were the moments that he was Alexander and Napoleon!

That was why he had been sorely tempted to reveal himself during that explosion between Scotty and Sinclair two days ago at rehearsal. He cherished and was proud of his restraint. Yet he was troubled, and the peace of the evening and the quiet river would not wash his brain clean of his worries. Why was the state trooper hanging around the theater? Why, why, when he accidentally came upon the trooper and Dr. Strong together, they so awkwardly yet so obviously talked of commonplaces

Despite the peace-inducing evening, Marc tormented himself by equating all members of the company with his own objectives. He could not isolate individuals from a possible involvement with the sinister implications of that damned letter. He methodically classified and evaluated each member of the company as well as people he had come to know in the community. Yes, there was a small group that had voiced its opposition to the intrusion of a decadent world into the bucolic peace of the community. But they were simple, sincere souls who would not harm the most reprehensible of humanity.

Marilyn, Sam, Dr. Strong—all were inoffensive. Joseph Jr.? He was really a problem. Marc revered the boy's father. He had been one of the independent and outspoken liberals in Hollywood. It sickened Marc to recall how the man had crawled before the congressional committee, how he sought out a role in the Broadway production of the drama based on the popular anti-Communist novel, *Midnight at Dawn*. The boy was very good-looking and with his name could become a popular actor. Yet, the deadly pattern in the theater, wherein the children of the great end up as drunks, dope addicts, and even as suicides, depressed Marc. How grateful he was that his son sought a career far removed from the theater.

Would it do any good, once the play opened, for him to have a talk with Joseph? Or maybe with his father? Cut it out, Marc! You've got one job—get that play on the best way you can!

Once embarked on taking inventory, Marc reflected on the others. He refused to think of Sinclair Turner. The man was not his type, and he had a bad taste in his mouth from his encounter with the man in Hollywood. Then there was Ellen. What was happening there? The girl had a talent—oh, not the kind that had a depth of weltschmerz so that he would cast her as Nina in *The Sea Gull*. But she could play with conviction and authority the wholesome Rosalind, even a Beatrice if sufficiently aroused by a Benedict with the proper amount of taunting abrasiveness. As she developed, she could conceivably grow into a role in a Noel Coward play, but definitely not in a Clifford Odets or Tennessee Williams drama. Yet, what was happening to her here and now? When she first arrived she had been so open, so eager as she sought him out for discussions of the theater as he knew it, as well as to discuss her role. She had been avoiding him. Why, she was even avoiding her old friend Sam.

Sam Dobrow. Marc could find no fault with him, yet he, too, was moodily immersed in some unreachable world where, Marc felt, he was intruding when he approached Sam about any large or small item concerning the production.

Was something going on about which he knew nothing? Again he quarreled with himself: Shmuck, you've got a job to get a play on; let it go at that and keep your nose clean. They're grown-up people and can look out for themselves. Grown-up people? For all her undigested Freudian diet, Marilyn behaved in a manner more normal and secure than that of any of them.

He stooped to pick up a dried branch, which he swished like a scythe at the tall grass on either side of the path. The viciousness with which he cut at the grass betrayed an agitation that vexed the tranquility of the evening. A voice brought him back to the moment.

"Too bad we have no windmills for you to joust with."

It was Dr. Strong. They exchanged greetings. Marc quickly thought that he must keep the doctor from going on ahead so that he not encounter Scotty and Valerie. Never one for small talk, Marc was relieved when his companion stood alongside him in contemplation of the river and spoke about the history of the spot on which they stood.

"All of us like to walk here, even though we know we're trespassing."

In response to Marc's puzzled rejoinder, he continued.

"Other than the country around the source of this river, oh, up in New Hampshire, this is probably the most picturesque spot—even Thoreau said so in his book about his journey on the Merrimac—and for almost a mile in each direction from us along the river, the land belongs to the Perkins family. But it's a benign proprietorship, for the natives have used it as their park for heavens knows how many generations with no interference from the Perkins family."

They walked a way back toward town and then stopped at a spot from where the vista was a Corot come to life. They paused to savor it. Marc ventured to say so.

"Interesting that you say so. That's been quite a controversy here. Some claim it for Constable, others for Ruisdael, but native American nonetheless. I'm a Cohen man myself. We had a New York artist by the name of Hy Cohen here one summer. He must have turned out fifty canvases, almost all from this very spot. I went to New York to see his exhibit at the ACA Gallery. Yes, he caught our little corner of the world here—with one exception."

He took his time to satisfy Marc's inquiring look.

"I've seen other works of Cohen, mainly watercolors, which are his forte. His oils, however, have a proletarian orientation. Something, I suppose, I've always associated with that gallery. Perhaps this town, this country, this world along our Merrimac closes out the turmoil of the urban, industrial life. All of Cohen's paintings of that summer fail to have one person in them. As though he was sucked in, despite himself, into a oneness with nature. Ah, and what nature! The paintings are not a superficial impressionism. You want to roll in the grass, you want to smell the flowers, you want to fling off your clothes and plunge into the river—that's how he painted these scenes. As though Thoreau was painting instead of writing."

"But the people here..."

"Yes, our people here. Do you know that we have three hundred and five registered voters here. What do you think of this for independent voters: in 1948 two hundred and eighty-three of them voted for Henry Wallace. And almost all of them are registered Republicans. They're Lincoln Republicans."

"How did Perkins vote?"

"I could guess. The current Perkins still bears a grudge against the town. You see, we once needed a new high school.

That was in his late father's time. The old man offered to finance it for the town provided the high school would be named after him. You know, Perkins High School. I was a youngster then, but I remember the fireworks in town about it. At the town meeting the old man was accused of having inherited his money from the old slave traders and mill owners who used to enslave the girls in the mills. Oh, I can tell you the passions were nasty. The town voted down accepting the money if Perkins's tainted name went with it. Now, the present head of the clan is willing to give this land to the town if it's named in perpetuity as Perkins Grove or Perkins Park."

"What do you think?"

"I'm not taking sides. If anything, I'm as pragmatic as many of the newcomers in this area. There's been a considerable influx of people from the cities into this area. I'd like to see this land accepted for a park by the town under any conditions before Perkins really becomes spiteful and sells it for subdivision into plots for hundreds of small homes."

"Is Lee Perkins related to these wealthy Perkinses?"

"Sort of, in a distant way, a poor relation. Now, that young man has talent, and his rich relatives should really help him. It seems that he wrote a poem thirty years after the fact about the Sacco-Vanzetti business. Of course the poem spoke of their innocence and martyrdom. You know, people around here still debate the matter, and the rich Perkins crowd was outraged by the poem."

"Seems to me the town should accept the name Perkins for this land; then, if and when Lee becomes a famous poet, the name would be associated with him and not the slave traders."

"You really don't know our town, its people, Marc. They will not do anything devious no matter how pragmatically wise or expedient."

They walked in silence until Strong added, "No one here believes Lee has all that talent. A matter of the prophet not being honored in his own country."

They walked slowly. Marc was grateful that it was still June and that no mosquitoes bothered him. He was also grateful for the companionship. Even if he weren't busy with the rehearsals and spending most of his nights blocking out the play that was to go into rehearsal immediately after this one opens, he couldn't think of one person in the company with whom he could carry on a conversation for long before it turned to that actor's egocentric world. Oh yes, perhaps Sam Dobrow, but he was busy with the sets and the actors and the lighting. Then, also, he had assumed that Sam would want any free time to be with Ellen. Again he had that gnawing uncertainty about her. The past few days she had been behaving strangely, almost mysteriously. The doctor's voice brought him out of his reverie.

"How about yourself? Do you like it here sufficiently to make your home here?"

"Too soon to make such a decision. By the way, I want you to know that you're doing magnificently in the judge's role. If I had typecast the role through an agency in New York or Hollywood, I couldn't have gotten any one better."

"You're very kind to say so. I certainly am not typecast. I've never seen myself in a position to judge my fellow man."

They had reached the end of the path where it joined a street with town arc lights. The ample, porched white houses with their black trim might have been a stage setting for an early American play. The doctor did not want to terminate the walk with Marc—perhaps he could draw him out about members of the cast and find a clue to the missing drugs. He admired Marc, but could he trust his own instincts about the director sufficiently to take him into his confidence? Wally had cautioned him to say nothing to anyone, simply to keep his eyes and ears open. Such dissembling was alien to the doctor.

Marc gave voice to his thoughts. "This street could be the setting for a play."

"Have you noticed the difference in the width of the clapboards on the houses?"

"Now that you mention it, yes."

"Well, the houses with the very narrow clapboards are at least 100 years old. The wider ones are from this century, sort of johnny-come-latelies. Most of the houses on the Main Street are the very old ones, from the 1700's."

"They really built them sturdy in those days."

"Yes, sturdy men and sturdy houses. It was a pioneer society. Work. No time for self-indulgence like the youth today. No cop-outs, cry-baby behavior, and this alienation nonsense, with the crutch of drugs."

That should get him talking, thought the doctor. It did, but not to give any clue.

When Marc thought back on this conversation after the tragic event that followed, he wondered at his own obtuseness.

"Life is very complicated and frustrating for young people today."

"How can you say that when you compare the formidable odds that confronted the pioneers. Oh, I suppose many of us romanticize about the simple life of yore. But let me tell you it was a life of unending drudgery—no electricity, no telephones, no hospitals, no . . . Oh, you can make your own list. Yes, I suppose after a week's work many of them sought oblivion by way of the rum bottle. But that did not serve to alienate them. They needed the relaxation, the oblivion to forget the massive tasks ahead, for one brief night in the week at most."

Let's get back on the track and out of the pulpit, thought the doctor. I'll get nowhere sounding off like this. Let's try a direct attack.

"I haven't noticed any drinking in your company."

"Is that a question? If it is, I can tell you that as far as I know, no member of the company is a drinker. You'll notice it after opening night when Davis throws his champagne party backstage for the company and the distinguished patrons. You'll see the actors gorging themselves with the food, but not liquor." Marc laughed as he continued, "I've never seen such compulsive freeloaders as actors."

"How sure can you be? Maybe one of them may be a hardened, secret tippler."

"Vergil Davis took no chances. He had enough sense to make certain on that score. Like any business, the theater is like a small village. Everyone knows everybody's business. You can be sure Davis checked very carefully. He has hopes of making this theater a permanent one for himself. He told me that he was extra careful in engaging a cast—you've yet to meet the jobbers who are coming up for the rest of the summer's repertoire—that was absolutely clean. You know, no homosexuals, no drunks, no drugs . . ."

At last! The doctor took his time as he reflected how to follow through. A squirrel stood immobile in their path. Dr. Strong interrupted Marc by calling his attention to it. When the squirrel scampered away, the doctor asked Marc to hand him the branch he was still carrying.

"Can you see the top of this tree? The light from the street lamp is just about enough. See that hole in the trunk just below the second branch from the top?"

"Yes."

"Now, just keep your eye on it."

The doctor started rhythmically to knock the branch in his hand against the trunk of the tree. Very soon, the head of a squirrel peeped out of the hole, and then the squirrel himself inquiringly came out and perched on the upper branch.

"Happens all the time."

Their walk continued. They were approaching the Main Street.

"You were saying that the company is clean, including those who are coming up. Davis undoubtedly knows their histories. But how about the young ones? When it comes to drugs, you never can tell."

"I suppose you never can really tell. But we're all thrown together so closely that if anyone in the company was on the stuff, it would get out pretty quickly."

"I've known some pretty closely knit families where they did not know that one of them was on drugs."

The doctor wanted to go through the roster of names in the company, but Marc's next words showed him how futile it would be.

"As far as I know, Dr. Strong, this company is as clean as any I've ever worked with. This town of West Endicott is safe from an infection."

The actors and crew all wore sweaters, or jackets, or long-sleeved shirts. How was the doctor to find any telltale signs on any of them? Perhaps at dress rehearsal he'll blunder into some dressing rooms. But he couldn't very well do it thoroughly because the female actresses may present a problem. Ah, he had it!

"Have you ever been to a clam bake?"

"No. It must be fun."

"Our volunteer fire department is having one at Endicott Beach. It would be a wonderful bit of relaxation, and fun as you say, for the company. Only two-fifty a head and that includes all the lobster they can eat. Plenty of free beer, too. The members of the company can bring their bathing suits and go swimming."

Dr. Strong's enthusiasm infected Marc who became excited about the prospects. This was, indeed, a piece of Americana that he, a city-bred kid, had never experienced. They parted after Marc promised to get the entire company to attend.

Dr. Strong walked away with nothing new to report to Wally. But if he would have met Marc a short time later, and if Marc would tell him about the new development, the good doctor would have plenty to tell Trooper Wally.

Concerned about Joseph's reliability on stage, Marc decided to cut out some of Joseph's speeches. With this in mind, he returned to the theater and went backstage where he would find his script. Alone in the theater, he found on Sam's desk the packages Vergil had brought from the town for Bobby Francis. Among them he saw the album of Noel Coward favorites. Of course he could easily allow Sam and Sinclair to select the musical interpolations. But, not wishing to be surprised at rehearsal and knowing that he must be authoritative and not appear to be directing off the cuff, he decided to listen to the album, make his selections, and give his instructions while buttering up Sinclair that he was grateful for the latter's suggestion and choice of Noel Coward. He found the turntable, placed the two discs from the album on it, and turned on the switch. Then he sat back to listen.

Among the numbers, "Mad Dogs and Englishmen" and "Mad About the Boy" recalled to Marc the first time he heard them in London—it was on his honeymoon. He grinned with nostalgic gratification when he heard Beatrice Lillie's "Party" number. "Bittersweet" soon had Marc singing the melodic chorus with the duet that ended the first side of the disc. Silence, and then the plop of the next record falling into place.

Instead of the Noel Coward medley continuing, Marc heard the unmistakable voice of Marlon Brando's Stanley Kowalski. Marc jumped up, stopped the machine, and read the label. It was blank. He turned on the switch and listened. The uncouth, gutter derived voice spoke.

"Whatsa matta? Don' ya know what's comin'? Dis play ain't gonna open—here or anyplace else. Ya some kinda dope or somepn? Yer lookin' fer trouble and yer gonna get it. So get wise to yaself an' clear outa here before it's too late."

The voice? It had a resonance that was familiar to Marc. Yes, he had heard many actors imitate Brando, that was easy enough. Yet that voice was someone he knew—but who? He played the record again and again, each time casting another person whom he knew in the role. Once he thought he detected the Brooklynese of Sam Dobrow; at another replay it could very well be the Bronxese of Vergil he so well remembered from years ago when they were young together and Vergil had another name. Each time he played the record, his concentration on the voice was distracted by the piling up of questions in his mind as to possible motives of each possible perpetrator of this ghastly prank. The only thing about which he was certain was that the voice was neither Lee Perkins nor Marc's wife. Neither was it that of any woman. Thus he could eliminate them from any connection with that confounded letter. Then again, might not any one of them have worked with another person, an accomplice? He could confront Lee Perkins. He could phone his wife. Even if they were the guilty one or ones, wouldn't any one of them deny it?

What to do?

On opening night, all Marc's fears, all his evasion of confrontation hit him with—*a murder*!

14

Break a Leg

No matter how many opening nights Vergil Davis attended, especially those of his own productions, and no matter how much he cynically sneered at the effete hangers-on of the theater who squealed across the lobby in greeting to other weirdos and queers who, like Dorothy Parker so aptly described, crawled out of the woodwork, he felt the apprehension and breathless anticipation of a sheltered virgin on her wedding night. For Broadway openings he usually exhumed a well-worn dinner jacket that he considered de rigueur for such occasions even though the lobby crawled with the widest variety of styles from smelly looking dungarees to bare-backed and deep-plunging décollatage and braless, provocative evening gowns. Opening night at the Town Hall of West Endicott provided the producer with a warm glow of accomplishment.

Curtain time had been advertised to be 8:30. When Davis drove into the parking lot behind the Town Hall at 7:30, he gleefully saw it to be already a third filled. He passed two Boy Scouts who were the parking-lot attendants and, waving a greeting to them, drove close to the stage entrance where he ignored the "No Parking" sign, turned off the ignition, and hurried through the stage door. A quick check there, and he then hurried to the front of the house to greet the subscribers and the handful of writers from the newspapers in the adjoining mill towns.

He found the scenery to be practically all in place, but Bobby was there with a brush in hand to add finishing touches here and there. Marilyn was sweeping the ground cloth, Dr. Strong was carrying a ladder off to the wings, Marc was adjusting the chintz curtains, while Dobrow quietly checked off items on the pad on his clipboard. All perfunctorily responded to the producer's cheerful greeting except a dour-looking Marc. Marc was in a faded blue sweatshirt and stained dungarees. Davis's face fell when he saw him.

"Hey, Marc. This is opening night. Why aren't you dressed for it?"

Marc scowled at him. "This is maddening. Minutes to curtain and that imbecile is still building the set. Wire New York! Get another designer or let me rearrange the theater and we'll stage the rest of the season in the round."

Davis laughed. "You've done a good job. I'm not worried so don't you be. How do you like my new, white dinner jacket?"

The director grinned weakly, "You look like a goddamned gigolo."

"We've got to give these hicks some class. Did you bring your tux?"

"No."

"Mine will fit you. You've got time to get over to my place and use mine."

"I'll see . . ."

"That's an order, Marc. You'll find the whole outfit. Now get going."

"Okay. First I've got some last-minute checking to do."

"Everything else shipshape?"

"I guess. But if you don't want to see a murder here, get that designer out of here."

"We'll discuss it in the morning. See you up front later. Break a leg."

He repeated the ritual of "break a leg" to the others and disappeared up the aisle to the front of the house.

Edging into the box office, he exchanged greetings with a

bespectacled young man who gently spoke to successive questioners.

"Sorry, we're sold out tonight. Tomorrow night? Sorry, that's sold out, too. We can take care of you tomorrow matinee or Sunday night."

Davis noted that some of them walked aside to consult with their friends and then rejoined the long line to buy tickets for future performances. He mentally rubbed his hands in glee. This was it! Just as he had anticipated. This was going to be a sensationally successful season. Not needed in the box office, he walked out into the small lobby where he saw a few early arrivals studying the pictures of the actors and posters of Vergil Davis Productions of past years with which he had decorated the walls that were painted with a neutral, institutional green. He smiled a greeting to a few who tried not to be surprised by his formal attire. Perhaps they expected it in show biz, for had they not seen the ringmaster in tails and white tie at the annual visit of the circus at Nashua?

The western sky was still gloriously light, as it should be this late June evening. It illuminated a heartwarming scene for Davis. Wally, the trooper, was directing a slow-moving line of cars in the road in front of the theater. Across the road, couples—the women in gaily colored, long-skirted party dresses—strolled aimlessly with their escorts for a peaceful smoke before entering the theater. Here and there on the lawn in front of the Town Hall, clustered like bunches of celery stalks, groups of well-dressed theater goers chatted in friendly relaxation.

The sight gave Davis renewed confidence in his astute sense of theater. He had selected this place because it was two hundred and fifty miles from New York, because within a radius of twenty-five miles there was a year-round population of over a quarter of a million souls who were starved for good, live theater. In making his rounds of the area, in talking with many people, he had found a high level of interest in the legitimate theater, in good books, in music—why, he had even had inquiries about the possibilities of modern-dance recitals at the theater. He expansively glowed and extravagantly projected his plans for future years. He would make this a cultural center for New England. He would establish an art colony here, have a resident music ensemble for a music festival. . . .

Backstage, Marc quickly reviewed last-minute details. He checked the lights with the tech man, screamed at Bobby to nail a picture over the fireplace, and heard Dobrow instruct Marilyn to go down to the dressing rooms to call the half hour. Then Dobrow barked at Bobby to clear his junk off the stage. Marc jumped off the stage to pick up his jacket that lay on a chair in the front row of the theater. Dobrow, alone on stage, took the gun out of his pocket and carefully placed it on the mantelpiece. Dobrow stepped back and was startled to find Joseph observing him.

"Will you check my makeup, Mr. Dobrow?"

"I'll be down in a few minutes."

Joseph turned to leave when Dobrow stopped him. "Here, do me a favor. Fill this decanter with water. Put it right here on the table."

Marc jumped back on stage and walked toward the exit. There, he turned to Sam. "You've checked the gun?"

Sam grinned at him as he nodded. "Break a leg."

"Break a leg. Draw the curtain and bring up the house lights. I'll tell them up front to open the doors."

He heard the soft swish of the curtain as he walked out into the gentle evening air. He resolutely walked up front into the lobby where he quietly instructed the ticket taker, a blonde youth who was a senior at the high school, to open the doors. Then, once again outside, he was stopped by Davis. They walked quickly toward the road.

"Try to hurry back, Marc. I want you to meet some of the important locals."

"I'll hurry. Don't worry. I was serious about the scene designer. We can try it once by giving a dramatic reading one week of *Don Juan in Hell*. It was a sellout in New York and on tour—with no scenery."

"Not without stars. With stars we can sell anything, but I'm not going to break my butt and give all the gravy to high-priced stars. When should I make my welcoming speech?"

Marc grinned, "Must you?"

"Yes, wise guy. It's customary and expected. Public relations stuff. This is the start of the season and they expect the producer to be chummy. Any more wise cracks from you and I'll drag you up in front of the curtain to make the speech."

"Well, I think the best spot would be after act 2 intermission."

Davis extended his hand to Marc. "Good luck, and thanks for everything."

"Yes, good luck to all of us. It's out of my hands now." And as he withdrew his hand, he sneered at himself, "My act of 'creation' is over."

"We're all proud of the job you've done."

"My job isn't quite done yet. I still want to clear up the mystery of why Sinclair Turner, of all people, was so anxious to be in a play I was directing."

"Because you're good and he knows it. He's a good actor and saw a good role for himself. Give him some credit for being a professional. So, you had him sacked. But a job is a job, so why should he bear a grudge?"

What Davis did not tell Marc was that, in order to make certain Sinclair would not entangle him with legal injunctions against presenting a play about the actor's private life, he had committed himself to an extra percentage for the actor in the production's limited partnership and had also given the actor a run-of-the-play contract if and when it would be produced on Broadway.

"It may be his conscience. I have a feeling he was the one who informed the congressional committee about me and got me blacklisted." Although Marc expressed himself quietly, his bitterness was all too apparent.

"He may be a heel, but I don't think he'd do anything that low."

"They called him, didn't they."

"Yes. But his evidence was in secret session."

Marc triumphantly stated, "There, that's it . . ."

"Hold on. You're usually such a nice guy. So, why not give the creep the benefit of the doubt? You've no proof. I never heard that he named names like so many other Judases did. If he had, it would have gotten around."

"How come he got such nice jobs after I was blacklisted? If I knew for sure that he did that to me, I'd kill him. So help me God, I'd kill him."

Giving Marc a bear hug, Davis tried to erase Marc's dolorous mood.

"Cheer up. You'll be able to write to your son and tell him that you can now start to write under your own name again. That's the wonderful thing about you creative artists—you can prove your worth sooner or later. Don't sneer at your gift of creativity. You'd be up the creek and still have a long way to go if you were just an actor or an interpretive artist in the same bind. So cheer up."

"You're assuming we're going to score with this play . . ."

"It's good, you know that. We all know that. If this one doesn't make it, I might as well quit and get out of the theater."

"There's still the big 'IF': *if* the public goes for it, *if* it's a hit on Broadway, and *if* it's sold to Hollywood. In other words, I can again become myself if others do things, no matter what I do."

"Cut it out. You've already done what you were supposed to do. And you've done it magnificently. I don't know how to talk to you. I don't know what to say to you anymore. Wait till you hear the applause after the final curtain, and read the rave reviews tomorrow. We've got the Boston critics tonight, you know."

Perhaps he had been too ungrateful to Davis. The producer

had really gone all out for him.

"I'm sorry, Verg. You've said all you could or should. I do appreciate what you've done. I suppose now that my part of the job is finished, I feel empty. Empty again. I've felt like that for such a long time that it's become a habit. Thanks ... for everything. Thanks for the chance you've given me. I don't mean just the chance to write this play, but the confidence you have in me. I can write ... I will write ... I've got so much stored up ..."

He was at the point of bursting with his enthusiasm that he became inarticulate. Realizing how corny he sounded, he caught himself and grinned while he extended his hand to Davis.

"Good luck to all of us. Good luck to my real self. Yes, I'm sure I'll be able to sign my own name from now on to everything I write."

"That's what I like to hear. Now hurry back. I've got to go back stage and wish them luck and give them these telegrams."

They parted company, Marc to dress and Davis to the stage door.

While bouyantly hurrying back toward the theater, Davis's thoughts raced ahead of him. They danced, danced in multitudes as they crowded his mind. He skirted the theater and saw with satisfaction that, during his few minutes with Marc, the parking lot had filled to three-quarters of its capacity and the crowds in front of the theater had multiplied. His spirits soared; instead of walking he felt as though he were being hurled upward by a trampoline. This was the spot he had dreamed of. Who knows, if the season succeeded half as well as he expected, he might even give up Broadway and make this his permanent theater and home.

What a revelation it had been thus far. On Broadway when he was in the throes of production, he had to devote most of his time, energies, and money to items and areas that had nothing to do with the artistic considerations of the play. He had to pay out, as all producers had to, large sums of money to unproductive "workers" who were protected in their featherbedded jobs by contracts imposed by unconscionable unions. Even though a one-set play had no music, had no changes of scene, had no costumes, nonetheless he had to add to his payroll musicians, stagehands, wardrobe mistresses, and—this particularly irked him—publicity agents, even though his own office staff could do the work perhaps better. In the 1930s he had mounted a one-set play on Broadway at a cost well below ten thousand dollars. Today it would cost over one hundred thousand and the cost was still rising. The one bright spot was the benign Actors Equity Association; the actors' union really understood the problems of the producer and the need to help keep the stage alive.

The first shock of surprise delighted Davis when he had learned that the stagehands unions would not make demands upon him to operate a strictly union theater. If they had insisted, his weekly operating nut would have doubled, thereby making survival most doubtful. If the public responded so that the theater made a little money, he would be able to offer a varied season of good plays from Shaw, Ibsen, even Chekhov, together with a few recent Broadway successes that the public expected. For next season he would establish a school for the apprentices whereby they would pay tuition while working around the theater in building sets and filling walk-on roles. Yes, he looked ahead to the time when Vergil Davis's name would be identified with one of America's really great theaters. He might take a flyer once in a while on Broadway, for one never knew which play might become another *Life With Father*; it, too, started in summer stock.

He hurried through the stage door.

The curtain was drawn, and the scene was lit by the standing lamp alongside the sofa. He saw Valerie at the mantelpiece where she was examining the gun. She quickly replaced it when she heard his greeting.

"Oh, Mr. Davis, have you seen Marc? I wanted him to check my makeup."

"He won't be back before curtain time. You look good to me, so what's the problem?"

"Is this enough eye shadow for act 1? Then, should I make it darker after act 1 to show how worried I've been?"

"Why not check with Sam? He knows what Marc wants."

"Shall I add any falsies."

"Mmmnn. I'm not sure. I think not—you look good to me. But do make the V deeper and add some shadow to the cleft. Good luck. You've come through magnificently. I knew you would ..."

He stopped upon seeing Everett come on stage. He quickly crossed to Valerie, took her hand and gallantly kissed it. Then he turned to the actor and shook hands with him.

"Thanks for everything, kids. Break a leg." Davis chuckled as he hurried off down the stairs to the dressing rooms.

15

Confrontation

Valerie turned with a bright smile to her former husband. Oh God, she thought, this would be a helluva time for me to start crying. His businesslike air calmed her.

"Hello," she heard him say.

"Hello."

"How do I look?"

She nodded approval. "Fine. Never looked better . . ." She caught herself, for she sounded too enthusiastic. This was a tricky time. No sense in emotionalism at this time. She quickly said, "Nervous?"

"No. And you?"

"I don't think so. I'm too dazed."

He reassured her, "I'm sure you'll be all right."

Silence. If each had known how the other was desperately hoping that the other would make one small gesture, would voice one wee word of encouragement, they would instantaneously be in each other's arms. Everett finally turned away from her and spoke in an all-too-obviously-calculated and matter-of-fact tone.

"This is the first time we're acting together since we were on the USO tour."

She silently nodded. He continued.

"Any plans after next week?"

"I don't really know. Davis says he's negotiating to have us tour some of the other summer stocks. They're waiting to see what *Variety* says. Meanwhile he may job me for a couple of weeks in *Candida*. Of course, if he actually does bring it to Broadway, the . . ."

"I wonder if it will ever reach Broadway."

"Maybe this is one of Davis's promises that will come true. He expects some prospective angels here tomorrow night. Some are here tonight with the man from *Variety*. And how about your plans?"

"No plans. No hopes, hence no plans."

"I'm sorry, Scotty."

"I want you to know that the walk we took down by the river was . . . well, I don't know, but I think I have never been so much at peace as I was there with you . . ." He awkwardly groped for the words that were rushing to be spoken.

"It won't do, Scotty. I hoped. I've constantly hoped that one day you would understand and finally believe me. There never was any one but you."

"I think I do believe."

This had been indeed hard for him to say, for it made everything he had done these past couple of years stupidly meaningless.

"Ah, Scotty. You really don't. You're saying it because of this situation we're in here, this propinquity, these close quarters of living in this microcosm of summer stock. It was inevitable that we would be thrown together as it might happen to any man and woman. But your problem is still there. Perhaps if you were helped, if you allowed yourself to consider psychoanalysis . . ."

His humble, helpless demeanor abruptly fled.

"I'm not your normal, smug, happily married shnook getting fat in a state of insensitive bliss. I don't sit home smoking my peaceful pipe, shod in house slippers after a hard day at my routine job. I don't putter around some postage-stamp-sized garden. I don't play a sociable game of bridge with some boring neighbors with whom I have nothing to say that would arouse them out of their intellectually impoverished lives.

Nor do I get stinko potted every Saturday night. I don't want to take my kid, if I had one, to the Little League. But I have emotions, a passionate belief in breathless, undying love—one love—soooo, I need straightening out, you tell me!"

"You might find some contentment—maybe we would. You act frantic most of the time. Your feeling of insecurity or guilt . . ."

"Guilty about what? I didn't hate my parents—consciously or unconsciously. Oh . . . I suppose you mean about shooting your . . . Sinclair. Yes, I do guilty. I feel guilty because I didn't kill him."

"You're killing yourself, and you won't face reality. There's still a chance, a hope for us if you would . . ."

"Join your congregation? Worship at the altar of the modern god, Adjustment? How often you've told me I don't face reality. Dreamer! Adolescent! You've told me that often enough. What's wrong with my adolescent dreams? Not a blessed thing. I defy any man to deny that the hopes and dreams of his adolescence weren't the most inspiring, intoxicating, brilliant, most magnificent unrealized adventures in his life. As I grow older, I don't propose to simper and smile apologetically as I indulgently sigh, 'Yes, I was young then—the dreams of my radical youth.' No, never. And I'll never apologize for those dreams nor dismiss them if I could. If any poor soul, when he reaches middle age, can say that he saw come true, that he realized the puniest, most infinitesimal one dream out of the more grandiose millions of dreams beyond his reach, from the hopelessly frustrating adolescent boyhood days of tortured delirium of near madness, if he could claim as real but the most insignificant of those dreams, then all our psychiatrists would have to go out of business. Of course, maybe that might have made me into the tolerant modern man, the single standard man, the man who is ready to accept his wife's 'friendship' with another man."

She shrugged helplessly.

"Hello."

It was Sinclair who had entered, unobserved.

Everett mumbled, "Speaking of the devil."

Valerie, hoping Sinclair had not heard, quickly offered her hand to Everett.

"Good luck, Scotty—tonight and always."

Sinclair excused himself by saying that he was just checking his props, upon which he crossed the stage and disappeared through the door that led to his stage bedroom. He returned immediately and addressed the other two.

"Good luck to all of us."

Only Valerie replied, "Good luck."

The other two looked expectantly at the mute Everett. Valerie reproached him.

"Scotty, this bitterness must end. The play may be a big success. Then we will be working together in New York for months—the three of us."

At first Everett silently looked away from them. Then he bestirred himself.

"I guess I'll check my props, too."

He busied himself in checking various items on stage. The other two shrugged helplessly and went down the stairs to their dressing rooms. Being sure that he was now alone, Everett quickly crossed to the fireplace, readjusted Sinclair's picture, and then picked up the gun. He examined it, held it a while, and when he heard someone coming up the stairs, he quickly replaced the gun and went out through the stage door to stand in the darkening evening. Out toward the west there lingered a deep orange and purplish hue. He looked along the length of the Town Hall and saw beyond its front the lighted lawn and the headlights of a long line of approaching cars.

Between Everett and the crawling lights, he saw the figures of Marc and that of Lee Perkins, who was everlastingly hanging around the theater. Had Everett been closer he would have heard their conversation.

"Yes, Lee, I read the play."

Lee eagerly questioned, "Yes?"

"I like it very much. But this is no time to talk about it."

"W-W-when would you suggest . . . ?"

"Come around after the performance tonight. We're having the usual opening party. Maybe, afterwards, we'll have a chance to talk."

Before Lee could offer his thanks, Marc continued, "Where were you going just now?"

"Oh, just back stage. I wanted to see Dr. Strong and wish him luck."

"Well, hurry. We don't allow anyone backstage during performance."

Marc turned to go, then impulsively questioned Lee, "You used the typewriter in the box office for your last act?"

"Yes."

"Did you use it for anything else, like writing personal letters or anything."

"Oh no. They were always so busy and needed the machine. I didn't want to be in the way. Oh no, I wouldn't . . . "

The protestations would have continued had not Marc stopped him with a curt, "See you later," as he abruptly walked away.

Soooo, schmuck, what did you accomplish? Thus Marc berated himself while he walked on. He was angry with himself for this futile exercise.

Back in the theater, onstage, Joseph had entered with the filled decanter, Sinclair came up directly after him and grabbed his shoulder just as the young man was straightening up from placing the decanter on the table.

"I saw you come out of my dressing room. What did you take there?"

Joseph looked at him sullenly. "Nothing."

"I don't believe you. What did you take?"

Silence. Sinclair closed in on him.

"Have your vocal chords failed or are you paralyzed by a fistula in your perineum? Don't just stand there as though you've got a ramrod shoved up your ass . . ."

The older man started to twist the youth's arm. "You'll tell me all right!"

Joseph squirmed in pain. He managed to gasp out at Sinclair, "I'll kill you for this."

They heard Dobrow on the stairs as the stage manager called out, "Ten minutes, everybody."

By the time Dobrow appeared, Joseph had disengaged himself from Sinclair who then hurried past the stage manager and mumbled, "Good luck."

"Good luck," replied Dobrow, and under his breath, "you bastard."

16

Curtain Going Up

The first act had been uneventful except that Joseph blew his lines once. Valerie ad libbed valiantly until the boy got back on the track. Perhaps he could not be entirely blamed, for the hum of excitement in the audience upon his first entrance was more than audible. Distinct words from the dark house could be heard: "Little Napoleon's son," and "not a bit like his father," and so on. Apparently Davis's showmanship instincts would pay off. But Marc, who had momentarily gasped when the lines were blown, was convinced that Davis should—must—give the young man his notice. There was something wrong there, and whatever it was would explode in their face; he was sure of it.

However, Marc sighed with relief while he stood at the back of the house. During the first intermission he allowed himself to be introduced by Davis to some of the local people. Their generous smiles, their genuine pleasure in meeting a "real director" may have seemed naive. But Marc liked them all the more for it; how different from the jaded sophisticates at New York opening nights, or in Hollywood for that matter. He graciously acknowledged their congratulations and their expressions of enjoyment.

Marc looked about him with hopes of espying the critics or some voluble people who might be commenting about the play. He walked past a couple who seemed to be in a heated discussion about the play. But when they saw him near them, they clammed up and smiled at him. "It's this damned tuxedo," he concluded. They associated him with the play and just wouldn't talk if he could overhear them.

During the second act Marc wanted to flee a million miles from the theater when Joseph stumbled through his lines. Dobrow did an efficient job of prompting, but Joseph seemed dazed and was slow to respond. Nonetheless, the others carried the act brilliantly while the audience probably thought Joseph's stumbling was part of the characterization.

"Two down and one to go."

It was Vergil Davis exultantly beaming at him.

"Get that lugubrious look off your face, Marc old boy. We're in—and big. I've heard nothing but praise—praise my eye—raves!"

Bully for him, though Marc. This is his moment, and that's as it should be: he's in the right spirit for his speech.

"All set for your speech, Vergil?"

"You bet. I'm just in the mood."

"I forgot to ask you. What'll you tell them?"

"Don't you worry. I won't destroy the mood of the play."

And Vergil vanished in the middle of a group, the members of which eagerly shook hands with him.

"Curtain going up," the nubile usherettes announced as they walked through the chatting, cigarette-smoking groups. The lights in the lobby and outside the theater blinked to punctuate their announcement. Marc took his place as a standee, the only standee, at the back of the house. The murmur in the audience subsided when the house lights slowly dimmed and the spotlight on the golden brown curtain gradually brightened. The expectant audience was completely silent now. Marc hoped Vergil would not be the flamboyant huckster. An urbane wit would help at this point in the evening.

The curtain parted, and Vergil Davis stepped forward into the spotlight. His face had a radiant, friendly smile. Someone in the audience clapped his hands in applause. Tentatively, a few others took up the applause and soon the applause was general, a polite kind of applause. With uncalled-for modesty and uncharacteristic diffidence, Davis raised his arms as a plea for the applause to stop, which it quickly did, perhaps too quickly for Vergil's liking. Pausing deliberately, Vergil stepped forward.

"Thank you, ladies and gentlemen. Let me introduce myself to those of you whom I've not had the pleasure of meeting. I am Vergil Davis. If you've done your homework and read your program, you will know by now that I am the producer. This will probably be the only time this season that I will appear before you onstage, so I'm going to make the most of it. Well, I started off by greeting you as ladies and gentlemen. You are all that, but I'd rather address you as friends and neighbors. When I first came to investigate the generous offer of your selectmen, cultured gentlemen every one of them, with a true affinity for the Arts, in which they offered me the use of this Town Hall, with its neo-classic architecture (y'know, they don't build 'em that way anymore), so that we could offer a summer repertoire of great plays, I was skeptical. Although I am dedicated to the art of the theater, I am a practical and conservative businessman. When I drove into town, the only welcoming committee to greet me was made up of a cow and a dog seeking cover from the cold March wind that blew me into town. All my life I had heard about New England reserve. Well, those animals showed it to me. They retreated after one disgusted look at this intruder from the big city. With their departure, I wondered where would I find an audience."

He paused in grateful acknowledgement of laughter that lightly rippled through the audience.

"*Mea culpa.* I confess to a condescending attitude: I looked upon myself as the anointed who was to bring culture, the great heritage of theater art, to a bunch of hick farmers. Please forgive me. Never was a man more mistaken than I. I have found here a citadel of culture, a haven of the humanities unequaled among the world centers where my meanderings have led me. I've been taught many lessons, I have been humbled. Humbled by your warm acceptance of me and my company, by your extraordinarily sincere and comforting welcome."

This had a ring of conviction to it, thought Marc. He's got me almost convinced. But, he's going on too much. It's time he wound it up. Vergil was just warming up.

"And the people here—everyone I've met—what can I say except to repeat how wonderfully welcome you've made us feel. I am determined to come back here for many years. Because you've all made us feel at home, I want to make this town my home."

Did he really mean all this? Gosh, to Marc he certainly sounded convincing. At last, thought Marc, he must be through—what else can he say except thank them again and urge them to come each week. Did David Garrick or Davenant make such curtain speeches?

"Thank you for your wonderful turnout tonight. Please tell your friends and neighbors that a real, a live theater, with professional actors direct from Broadway, is flourishing here. Come back each week with them to see our new plays. We offer you the latest hits from Broadway in their original, uncut version—the honest article, and not like the cut-up and expurgated versions you get in the films from Hollywood. We also bring you the great classics of the ages, plays by Shaw, Ibsen, Chekhov, Miller, Tennessee Williams, and so on. We hope to establish a center of culture here. Once again this region will be known as the Athens of America. Grandiose dreams? No! We are determined to realize this dream, to make it live. We want you to be proud of us as we are of you. Thank you for being a wonderful audience. Please stay after tonight's performance for a reception on the lawn. Our actors want to meet you. And now, on with the play—the last act! Thank you."

With his hands aloft like the successful nominee at a presidential convention, Vergil Davis acknowledged the respectful applause from a grateful audience. His moment of glory over, Vergil Davis bowed and exited through the fold of the curtain. The spotlight dimmed, and the theater was in complete darkness and utter silence.

When the lights came on again, Valerie was seen in her room, down front on stage left, with a scrim behind her. She was discovered talking on the phone.

"I'm at the end of my rope . . . Dress rehearsal is tomorrow night . . . yes . . . I told Scotty I'd do anything. Yes, of course, I'll break my contract, I'll give up the stage . . . anything . . . oh, I'll get some kind of job, but that's not the answer. Scotty is proud, he's got to be the breadwinner, head of the family . . . No, that won't do. You should have seen how he exploded when I only hinted that you might help. He doesn't want anything from anyone, even though you are my brother . . . Especially from you, he says . . . That's the point, you can't reason with him. I just can't get through to him any more . . . He left, oh, I guess it must have been an hour ago. He threatened to kill Turner. I'm so frightened. I've been trying to get Turner on the phone, but the phone is out of order . . . I'm going out of my mind . . . I just don't know what to do . . ."

The lights faded down. When they came on again, the scene was Turner's room behind the scrim. Sinclair Turner and Ellen discovered alone. Ellen was enraptured as Sinclair walked about while she sat at the edge of the sofa, eagerly listening to his every word.

"You have to understand that there is no generalization nor method in acting that is a substitute for talent. The Stanislavsky method is for actors who have no talent."

He paused and turned to her with a smile of simulated awe and sincerity.

"You have that talent."

The smile on his face gave way to a look of humble admiration as he made a bow from his waist with his arms stretched out and downward. She gasped incredulously, but quickly recovered her intense excitement in the exchange with him.

"But I was taught that one must live the role ... it's the only right way to ..."

He came toward her as he spoke with the conviction of professional authority.

"So ... to play Anna Christie you have to go out and really be a prostitute, eh? Nonsense. Let me show you the living-the-role technique in that beautiful scene from Romeo and Juliet."

Sinclair made a big to-do about finding a copy of Shakespeare in his bookshelves. He riffled through its pages.

"Ah, yes. Here it is, act 3, scene 5. Let's take, for example, Juliet's opening speech. I'll recall it to you. She has just awakened after spending her nuptial night with her beloved Romeo. How would you start the scene? Would you plunge into her rapturous, lyrical speech at once?"

Ellen did not respond at first. When he again asked, "Would you?" she desperately shrugged, then spoke.

"That depends on the entire concept, how the director wanted it played."

"Very well, let's suppose he's of your mind, the 'method' concept and really living the role."

As he read, he demonstrated with yawns, gargles, belches and blowing his nose at the appropriate spots in the speech:

"She might yawn first, rise, scratch her behind like so ... and then start,

Wilt thou be gone? It is not yet near day.
It was the nightingale and not the lark
That pierc'd the fearful hollow of thine ear ...

and so on and so on ...

"Now, what is Romeo doing meanwhile? He's got to beat it out of town or his life is forfeit. So, we hear him in his matutinal ablutions . . . he's gargling, then a loud belch, like me . . . [belches] and then, while he yawns, he speaks to her,

It was the lark, the herald of the morn.
No nightingale. Look. love, what envious
streaks do lace the severing clouds in yonder
East, . . .

and so on and on and on. . . ."
"Yes," she laughed, "it does seem absurd. But different plays demand different treatment, different styles."
Reluctantly, as though waiting for her cue for which he had been preparing, he closed the book and walked toward the shelves. At last she said what he had been hoping she'd say.
"How would you interpret the scene?"
"First, I'd need a Juliet . . ."
"I'll be delighted to read with you,"—he could have written it!
"I couldn't dream of a better Juliet. You see, you don't merely take my word cues and respond to them. You respond to the mood of the other actor or actors, no matter how much you are living within your own shell. All right, let's start . . ."
He sat beside her on the sofa and started to read the rest of that scene from *Romeo and Juliet*. Unobtrusively, while the reading proceeded, Sinclair gradually placed his arm around Ellen's shoulder. At the line, ". . . *Farewell, farewell! One kiss and I'll descend,*" he put the book aside and took Ellen in his arms and kissed her. She fervently responded. Then she rose and crossed to the window at her left. He followed. She did not look but was aware of him by her side as she spoke.
"How lonesome the gulls hover out there."
"How often I've been lonesome, here, alone, listening to them unseen over the soft, dim mist of the river."
She turned to him with a shy smile, "And how . . . ?"
"I'm not lonesome now. You're here. Oh, my darling, how I've wanted you here, beside me. Now . . . now can I ever be

lonesome again . . . Here, secluded in our temporary abode, we seek . . ."

My God, gasped Marc to himself as he heard Sinclair, did I write that saccharine drivel? Yet, damn it, it sounded convincing. Despite the lines about Sinclair's antipathy to "living the part," by God he most certainly was living this part. And she, Ellen, she fitted into his arms as though she'd been there before . . . and not on stage . . . as though she had a proprietary right to be there. Poor Sam, gulped Marc.

Meanwhile, on stage, Sinclair and Ellen were tenderly in each other's arms. Sinclair was masterful in the scene. He managed to convey a bursting, intense passion under control of the urbane, enlightened male. Even Marc responded with a stirring sensuality. It had the aspects of sacred and profane love united in supreme consummation. As he groped for his words her body became one with his. He lifted her in his arms, kissed her again, and carried her through the door to his bedroom.

The stage remained dark for a minute when the phone rang. The lights came up, and Sinclair, without his jacket and tie, with open collar, hurried in. He took the phone receiver off the hook and placed it alongside the phone on the table. He turned down the table lamps and then exited into the bedroom.

The audience laughed as the stage became completely dark to indicate the passage of two hours.

17

An Unexpected Ad Lib

On the whole, Marc was gratified with the audience reaction. He was particularly pleased at the laughs he had hoped would come at certain moments—and they did. He had been furiously making notes all over his program, and then he found some envelopes in the pocket of his jacket and filled both sides of three of them with his notes. Of course he could have had a pad on his clip-board, but it would have looked too obvious and artsy to anyone from the audience who might have spied him. Admittedly, his notes were critical only of minor details such as the position of a chair, the timing of a light cue, the waiting for a laugh to subside, and curtain timing. During the first two acts he went through the motions of making most of his notes about Joseph, although he knew all too well that a session with the boy in reviewing the notes would be useless, fruitless.

But, thus far, on the whole, it was a professional production, and the audience seemed tensed for the denouement.

The lights went up on the same scene, two hours later. Sinclair is discovered seated alone on the sofa. He was comfortably dressed in a pair of slacks, house slippers, and open shirt. He was reading a magazine and sipping a highball. His record player was playing Noel Coward's "I'll See You Again," when his doorbell rang. He rose, turned off the machine, crossed to the door, and opened it. Valerie stood at the door.

"*What a welcome surprise. Come in.*"

She entered with her nervous greeting, "*Hello, Mr. Turner.*"

"*You look upset.*"

"*I tried to get you on the phone. It's out of order.*"

Sinclair guiltily crossed to the phone and replaced the receiver on its cradle. He helplessly turned to her.

"*It's my cleaning girl. She must have knocked it off the cradle and simply didn't have sense enough to replace it. It's tough to get efficient help these days. As careless as she is, I'm lucky to have her. I'm sorry you couldn't get me. But I must admit I'm glad you didn't. It brought you here in person. It must be very urgent.*"

He added the last when he noted her discomfort at his attempt at gallantry. She was having a bad time trying to start to tell him what she had intended.

"*I've got to talk to you. It's very difficult. I just don't know . . .*"

"*Relax. Sit down and let me get you a drink. You've got to take care of yourself, be in good shape for our opening night.*"

"*No, thank you. I can't stay. I mustn't stay.*"

"*I want to help you if I can.*"

"*You've been very kind. I know I owe my part in the play to you. You've been so very helpful in every way.*"

"*Don't give it another thought. I'm very selfish about these things. When it comes to the theater, I want to be associated only with the best. You've got a great talent. A talent like yours is very rare. I needed you to play opposite me. Now I'm afraid, I'm sure of it, you're going to steal the show.*"

She smiled weakly as she made a gesture of helplessness.

"*You're so kind . . . it's difficult to talk to you.*"

She rose and walked halfway toward the window, then turned and spoke with resolution.

"*I can't go on. You must get my understudy to take over my role.*"

He started to say something, but she frantically interrupted him.

"Believe me, it's the wisest thing ... the only way. I've given this a lot of thought. I know how you ..."

He wouldn't let her go on. "Impossible! There's no way of doing it without you. It's unheard of. I refuse to listen to this nonsense ..."

"You might as well know the score. It's Scotty, my husband. He's a wonderful person, really. And I love him more than anything in the world."

"You mean that business with the flowers when I ..."

"Please don't judge by that. You were sweet and thoughtful. I'll never forget you for it."

"Scotty's a good actor. I saw him last season in that off-Broadway thing he was in."

"That's almost a year ago. He hasn't had a thing since. Can you imagine what it's done to him. He's desperate."

"If we get good notices, he can read for the road company. I'll put in a good word ..."

She interrupted him, "That's not the point. Right now it won't help."

She paced back and forth in her anxiety and wondered how to explain her intimate problem to him. She sat helplessly, avoiding his gaze.

"He's been brooding and thinking all sorts of things, awful things. He's ... he's terribly jealous."

"I'm sorry. It could be sticky."

"I'm afraid of what he might do. He's threatened all sorts of things. He's completely irrational."

"Has he seen a doctor? It seems to me ..."

"You mean psychiatry. Yes, he needs it."

Sinclair tried to help her out of her agitation, "Don't we all."

"I've suggested it to Scotty. my brother offered to pay for it. When I bring up the subject, he gets angry. But that isn't why I came. He's become worse. I mean ... he's been threatening all sorts of things. I'm afraid of what he may do. I don't know ... I've never seen him so wild ..."

Her desperate recital exhausted her control. She started to

weep. Sinclair sought some means to comfort her. He walked toward her and placed his hand on her shoulder to calm her.

"Come now, it's all going to be all right. After the play opens, your days will be free and you'll be able to spend time with him, to devote your thoughts to his problems. Right now you must clear your mind of all worries, think only of your role in the play, and be ready for opening night."

She walked away from him and pleaded.

"You don't seem to understand. You mustn't count on me ..."

"Nonsense. You've got a responsibility there, to everyone connected with the play. More important, you've got a responsibility to yourself. You can't ruin yourself that way. Now you just listen to me ..."

"You've got to understand. Scotty's been making threats. He says he's going to ... to ... to harm anyone he sees talking to me."

"He'll be all right and so will you once the tensions of opening night are over and behind us. I'm counting on you, we're all counting on you to come through like a real trouper in this play ... not just for me but for the cast, for everyone ... especially for yourself."

He finished his drink and refilled his glass from a bottle of scotch and with water from the decanter. He downed the drink in one long gulp, and then refilled his glass with the same and sipped while he talked.

"Now you just let me handle him. I'll get in touch with Scotty and ask him to have lunch with me tomorrow."

Valerie started to protest, but he waved her prostestations aside.

"I'll talk with him and everything will be all right. God's in his heaven and all's right with ... Here, have some of my drink."

"No, thank you. I've got to get home in a hurry. That's just it. He'll be wondering where I am if he gets in and doesn't find me.

"Well, cheers." He drank again. "*A long and happy career, on the stage and in your marriage.*"

"I can't see how your talking to Scotty will help. He doesn't want anyone to patronize him."

"You worry too much. Just leave it to me. At the very least, it's worth a try. From what you tell me, my talking to him can't make anything worse. So just don't worry yourself . . ."

Apparently the intense drinking had begun to have its effect on Sinclair. His movements became broad and his speech slurred. He made an effort to comfort Valerie by placing his arm around her shoulder. In her woeful state she thought nothing of his gesture and accepted it. Suddenly the door burst open—Scotty stood there.

Sinclair cheerily greeted him. "Come in, Mr. Scott. We were just talking about you."

He saluted Scotty with his drink, which he finished off. Everett silently crossed the threshold when Valerie stopped him.

"What are you doing here?"

"I caught you. That's what I'm doing here. I followed you. I knew you'd come to your . . . your . . . lover!"

Sinclair bestirred himself. "See here, Mr. Scott. I don't know what your personal problems are, but you're being very unfair to Valerie. She's opening in a couple of nights in a play that's sure to make her the greatest star in our theater. You're upsetting her, driving her frantic when you should be helping her, encouraging her to think only about her role, about the play."

"My wife's protector! I know all about you. I know how you get actresses to play opposite you, what they have to do."

Everett pointed to the sofa, "Is that your casting couch?"

Valerie pleaded with him. "Please, Scotty, please. Let's go home."

She tugged at him in her desperation to get him to leave. He brushed her aside.

Sinclair disgustedly turned away from him. "*Don't give me*

any corny lines from some tawdry melodrama you've been in."
Everett stalked him. *"I know why she's here with you . . ."*
Sinclair refilled his glass and then another.
"You're out of your mind. Go home and sleep it off. Here, have a nightcap with me. I'll tell you what. How about meeting me for lunch tomorrow and we can talk everything over calmly like grown men instead of hysterical kids?"
Sinclair filled his glass with water from the decanter while Everett hurled a tirade at him.
"You're right. I'm out of my adult mind. But of course I've no right to be. Absolutely not. I simply find my wife in a man's apartment. He has his arm around her. Who is this man? He only has the reputation of being the town stud, so why should it bother me if she's alone with him? After all, he's not an ordinary man. He's a great star. Hence, I should be honored. What if he has his arm around her? Maybe she's only dazzled by the great star. Maybe it's only a rehearsal . . ."
Everett walked about the room. He pointed to the mementos over the fireplace. Everett picked up the picture of Sinclair in uniform.
"Picture of the great star in his country's war effort. My, how handsome in uniform. And medals! Medals for the bedroom warrior."
Everett had been picking up and replacing the items he had been naming. Now he picked up the gun.
"And this gun . . . did you capture it or did you buy it in a Bowery pawnshop like you probably bought these medals?"
He now held only the gun and soberly looked at it. He was about to replace it, then he turned with the gun still in his hand, to Sinclair.
"Next time I see you, Sinclair Turner, I, too, will have a gun. I'm going to kill you, like so . . ."
Everett aimed the gun at Sinclair and pulled the trigger. The gun exploded. A dazed Sinclair staggered, weaved about, and fell to the floor.
Valerie screamed while Everett rushed toward Sinclair.

An Unexpected Ad Lib 145

"Everett ... What have you done ... !"

While Everett kneeled over the fallen actor, Valerie sank down beside him and lifted his head to her lap. Silence. From the wings, the stage manager hissed out the words as he prompted the next speech to Sinclair.

"I'm hit. Get a doctor ..."

There was no response from Sinclair. Dobrow tried again.

"I'm hit, get a doctor ..."

Silence.

A dazed, stupefied Valerie rose. She turned first frantically to Everett and then screamed to Dobrow, "He's dead."

Dobrow tried again. He could not comprehend the reality of her words.

"I'm hit, get a doctor ..."

Valerie stumbled toward the wings, "But he's dead ... really dead!"

Everett tried shaking Turner while Valerie continued. "He can't say his lines ... he's dead ..."

She turned back to Everett, "Oh, Scotty, what have you done ... ?"

Everett was frantic. "What's going on here?" He tried shaking Sinclair again. "Stop clowning, Turner ..." He screamed at the fallen actor, "Turner!"

He still held the gun as he rose and staggered toward Valerie.

"How did it happen? It must have been loaded with a real bullet ... Oh my God!"

Dobrow came on stage with the script in hand. Valerie turned to Dobrow, "Pull the curtain. Quick, get a doctor! Where's Dr. Strong?"

The audience was thrilled with the realism of the scene. An electric excitement was being generated from the stage. One member of the audience was puzzled; he was Wally, the Trooper. He knew from his conversations with Dr. Strong and from what he had read in the local papers that the actors were playing their real-life roles. But he did not recall that the town's own Dr. Strong was incorporated into the play's action. Dobrow, loudly calling for Dr. Strong, rushed off stage and quickly the curtain was drawn. The applause was spontaneous and loud. Dobrow stepped before the curtain and held up his arms to quiet the audience. But the applause continued. Dobrow bellowed out to them.

"Please, stop, please, ladies and gentlemen ..."

Marc had rushed down the aisle, jumped up on the apron and disappeared through the center fold of the curtain. Dobrow continued to beseech the audience.

"I'm sorry, ladies and gentlemen. There's been a terrible accident ..."

He was interrupted by a few laughs which soon spread through the audience.

"I mean it. Please, is the state trooper out there? Wally, are you there?"

Wally was urged by his wife to go on stage. He was mystified and reluctant. When he arrived on stage, Dobrow earnestly told him, "This is not the play. Something went wrong. Turner has really been shot."

The trooper immediately took over. He turned to the audience.

"This looks like the real thing. You better all stay put."

A distraught Davis ran down the aisle and jumped up on stage alongside the trooper.

"Please, everyone please remain seated. Everything will be all right."

In the next morning's *Boston Tribune*, the drama critic repeated Vergil Davis's plea and added, "By that time it was too late, for most of the discriminating theatergoers had already left this turkey after the first act."

Davis's voice was not reassuring, despite his forced smile with which he tried to beam his confident authority at an audience by now thoroughly bewildered. Quickly stepping back through the break in the curtain's center, he turned to see Dr. Strong kneeling beside the body of Sinclair Turner.

The doctor solemnly raised his head and made the quiet and awed announcement.
"He's dead."

18

An Actor's Role

The trooper had taken over. In a matter of minutes he had the corpse covered with a piece of canvas, had the stage manager put on the house lights, and had stepped before the curtain to talk to the now noisy audience.

"I've deputized Mr. Davis and Mr. Denis to make certain no one leaves the backstage area. It would help us if you will please remain in the theater . . ."

A voice from the audience interrupted him. "I'm a reporter. Can I go up front and call my paper?"

"O.K. But first call my headquarters and tell them there's been a homicide. Tell Chief Andrews to get here right away, and tell the constable who's directing traffic to check anyone who leaves the theater."

The reporter ran up the aisle with a determination that ill-concealed his excitement. The trooper went back behind the curtain. The audience was in a state of uncontrolled agitation. Many of them ignored the no smoking signs and gathered in groups in the aisle. None left the theater even to relax in the small lobby. Each eagerly waited for word from backstage. They had actually seen a murder committed? A moralist might be inclined to pass judgment upon the morbid curiosity of people who wait to see the outcome of a tragedy. But the drama was certainly compelling for the populace of this otherwise peaceful community.

When the trooper stepped behind the curtain, he found a stunned group. The doctor was earnestly talking with Marc Denis. Everett was in a state of shock as he sat helplessly on the sofa with Valerie over him, her comforting hand on his shoulder as she tried to reassure him. Everett looked up at the trooper.

"The gun was supposed to have only blanks in it." He still held the gun in his hand with an illogical fascination.

"Hand it over."

The trooper took the gun from the hapless actor by holding it at the open end of the barrel, took out his handkerchief, wrapped the gun in it, and placed it in his pocket.

"I assume there are blanks in it yet. But some joker must have put one real bullet in it. That person could have been you."

"I didn't. I wasn't anywhere near the damned gun until I had to use it in the scene when I shot it ... Oh, my God ... "

He wrung his hands while Valerie tried to soothe him.

The trooper turned to the stage manager. "Mr. Dobrow."

Sam had been trying to extricate himself from a garrulous Marilyn who had been hurling theories at him about all those who had motives to murder Sinclair. He gratefully turned to the trooper.

"Mr. Dobrow, that scene you and Mr. Turner were rehearsing last week ... Do you remember it?"

Marc interrupted, "Mr. Dobrow is not in the play."

"Let Mr. Dobrow speak for himself. And when I ask anyone a question, only that person is to answer. Now, Mr. Dobrow, you remember the day I brought you the gun permit?"

Sam thought a moment. "Oh, that. It wasn't a scene from this play at all. You know how actors are. We were discussing certain methods of acting."

"You threatened to kill Turner. You mentioned his own name. Just exactly what play were you rehearsing?"

"I don't actually remember. There were a few of them all jumbled up."

"Try to remember which plays they were. I'd suggest you'd better do some real concentrating."

The two men stood quietly looking at each other. Sam avoided looking toward Ellen, then he brightly looked up.

"Oh yes, we had been discussing the confrontation between characters in different plays and how one will react to the threat of another character. Turner said he was trying to play his role with dignity, but was having a helluva time when Everett threatened him. So we pretended that I would threaten him, as though it were in real life, and then see how he would react. That's all there was to it."

"Did you check the gun before the play opened tonight?"

Before the stage manager could answer, Dr. Strong asked him to wait a moment while he drew the trooper aside. Making certain no one would overhear him, the doctor spoke earnestly to the trooper. The trooper reached into his pocket to take out the gun, but the doctor stayed his hand. The trooper then looked around at all the others on stage, and with a smile, nodded at the doctor. Then he walked around the stage inspecting the various props and furniture. Taking his stand near Sinclair's table, he again turned to Dobrow.

"Well, Mr. Dobrow. Did you check the gun before the play opened?"

"Yes."

"What time was that?"

"It must have been five after eight."

"What makes you so sure of the time?"

"Ask Marc."

The trooper turned to Marc with an inquiring look. Marc answered.

"I remember. I asked him to make a routine check of the props. I assume that included the gun. He says he checked it."

"But you didn't see him do it?"

"No."

"Then he could have tampered with it. Like, for instance,

substitute a real bullet?"

Sam heatedly was about to respond when Ellen blurted out, "That's ridiculous . . ."

The trooper turned to her and said, "You'll have your chance to say all you want to later."

Ellen looked helplessly at Sam as the trooper relentlessly continued.

"Let us assume you merely looked at the gun to make certain it was in order. Could anyone have tampered with it after you checked it out as being in order?"

"No one is supposed to."

The trooper impatiently growled, "No one is supposed to go around shooting people either. Please answer the question. Could anyone have done it?"

"I suppose so. Usually I don't allow anyone onstage or allow anyone to touch anything once the scene is set. But this is opening night, lots of confusion, people coming and going all over the place. I tried to stop them, but I couldn't be everyplace at once. Let me see, I was downstairs before curtain time for at least ten minutes."

"Where downstairs."

Sam remained silent. The trooper impatiently stared at him. Finally Ellen spoke.

"He was with me."

"Let me ask you another thing, Mr. Dobrow." The trooper hesitated, looked at Ellen, and then directed his question. "You didn't like the . . . Mr. Turner, did you?"

"I don't know anyone who did."

"Hey, just a minute . . ." It was Marc who appeared troubled about something as he stepped forward and looked around at all of them as though he were taking stock. "Where's Joseph?"

It was Marilyn who volunteered the answer. "He was down in his dressing room when I last saw him."

"Get him," the trooper instructed her. Then he thought better of it. "No, stay here with everyone else. Doc, please get that kid up here."

Before the doctor moved, he addressed everyone on stage. "I've covered the body. Nobody go near it. The chief will probably bring the coroner."

Confident that Wally would make certain that his cautioning words would be heeded, the doctor quickly went down the stairs to fetch the young actor.

Those who remained on stage were mute figures in a tableau of expectancy, except for Davis who paced about. Suddenly he whirled and wildly shouted at all of them.

"One of you degenerates murdered Sinclair Turner. This means ruin for me, ruin for all of us. You murdered one of the greatest chances we all had to make it big. Ruin, that's all that faces us." He turned to the trooper and screamed with venomous, vengeful invective, "When you find that son of a bitch, I don't care who it is, I personally want to pull the electric-chair switch."

Davis ripped off his black tie and stiff collar, flung it at the fireplace, and slumped defeatedly into a chair. Marc shook his head and threw up his hands in doleful resignation. The silence that followed Davis's outburst seemed interminable when Marilyn excitedly started to splutter.

"Maybe somebody in the audience shot him. There's no proof it was a bullet from the gun. Someone in the audience, maybe in the wings, or outside through one of the windows in the auditorium, could have timed the shot simultaneously with Scotty's shot."

The trooper smiled indulgently at her. "Our ballistics department will check all that."

Encouraged by his respectful response, she continued.

"I was right there, standing next to Sam. I saw the whole thing. Will I be a witness? Gosh, I'll never forget this till I die. Wait'll I snow them when I get to college . . . Wow!"

Once again, the trooper turned to Sam.

"Now, Mr. Dobrow, do you want to say anything else at this time?"

"We all know this is a terrible situation. But aren't you supposed to make the routine statement yourself about 'anything I say may be held against me, that I am supposed to know about my rights, get benefit of counsel, make a phone call for my lawyer,' and all that jazz?"

"You're not under arrest . . . yet."

"I didn't do it. And that's that. Arrest me if you want to."

"I heard you threaten Turner last week. You were the last one to check the gun. You were responsible for the gun. That means you had the motive and the opportunity. I wouldn't like to be in your boots."

Ellen defiantly came to Sam's side. "Sam didn't do it. He couldn't have done it."

"You seem so sure about that, don't you, Miss Everhope? Suppose you tell us what makes you so sure."

"Yes, I'm sure. I'm sure that Sinclair committed suicide . . ."

She faltered, then started to weep. She ineffectually tried to control her tears and to speak calmly, but the more she tried, the more she wept.

". . . and it's all my fault. He said he'd kill himself if I didn't marry him. I told him I didn't love him. He was such a lonesome person. Everyone hated him. He needed understanding. I tried to be kind to him. He said no one ever spoke so . . . so friendly to him. He said he needed me . . . and I . . . I drove him to his death."

"Very interesting set-up. You're suggesting that the deceased put the bullet into the gun himself . . ."

Everett came to life. "And then he could get me convicted for killing him." He laughed incredulously. "You know, I wouldn't put it past him. What a ham thing to do."

Now the trooper turned to Everett again. "Mr. Scott, it is conceivable that you inserted the real bullet, you know."

In response, Everett shrugged his shoulders. But Valerie insisted, "I was near Scotty all the time. He couldn't have done it. The entire audience was watching him all the time, too."

As though it were a new thought that came to him, the trooper asked Valerie, "Miss Walker, were you on stage alone before the opening curtain?"

"Yes."

Everett roused himself quickly. "I was with her. She wasn't near the gun."

"You both could have . . ." The trooper was interrupted by the entrance of Dr. Strong leading Joseph. The doctor was upset.

"This boy has to get to a hospital."

"I'm all right," Joseph howled out. He saw Everett and rushed at him. "Why did you hate him? All of you. You had no right shooting him just because you didn't like him. He was the only friend I had. He meant more to me than that father of mine . . ."

The front curtain parted and the reporter came onto the stage.

"They're on their way," he told the trooper. "The constable and a trooper in a prowl car are watching up front. Oh, here are a bunch of telegrams they gave me in the box office to give to Mr. Davis."

Davis roused himself and stepped forward to claim them. But the trooper waved him back with the words, "I'd better take them for now."

The producer tried to assure him, "They're probably only congratulatory telegrams for members of the company. All harmless."

"Probably are. But I better hold them till I get orders."

Joseph insistently asked the Trooper, "Is there one for me?"

The trooper hesitated a moment, then said, "I guess there's no harm in finding out." He riffled through the telegrams. "Yes, it's from Westwood, California. I'll read it if you wish me to."

"Yes."

Selecting the one and placing the others in his packet, the

trooper read, "Congratulations and best wishes. I'm with you all the way. Signed, Dad."

To the surprise of everyone, Joseph snarled, "Why isn't he here ... he should be here. I wish he were lying there dead instead of poor Sinclair."

Marilyn led him aside.

The trooper went through his routines with the usual cliché by asking anyone who knew who did it to speak up, otherwise such a person would be guilty of being an accessory. Marc became impatient with him.

"Neither the one who did it nor the one who may know will confess just because you ask him ... or her ... to do so."

Sheepishly, the trooper confessed, "I don't know. I have never been on a homicide case before. But it seems to me that if the murderer confessed so soon after the deed, like right now, it would eliminate the business of premeditation. He would still seem to be under a terrific strain ... you know, sort of temporarily out of his mind. That means he wouldn't be tried for first degree. It may save him from the electric chair."

He looked around uneasily. He wished t'hell the chief would arrive. What should he do now? He was getting more and more uncomfortable. Should he keep them standing around? No sense in that.

"I'll ask you, Mr. Scott, and you, Mr. Dobrow, to stay right here. The chief should be here right away. Meanwhile the rest of you can go to your dressing rooms, you can change if you wish. But be ready if we want you up here ... "

Valerie gasped out, "Scotty couldn't have done it."

Ellen agreed, "Of course he couldn't. It was suicide. Sam didn't do it, I'm sure."

Everett hastened with his contribution, "I easily could have done it, except I didn't."

"Shake, pal." Dobrow offered his comment. "I'd gladly have done it. Only I didn't."

"Well, we'll see," said the trooper. "Maybe you both conspired to kill him. Both of you just stay put."

"Scotty didn't do it. I know."

Oh no, groaned Marc to himself. Here it comes, the Joan of Arc bit. Apparently the Trooper had seen the same movies.

"O.K. I'll bite. How do you know, what makes you so positive, Mr. Scott is innocent?"

"Because I did it. I put in the real bullet."

"That's fine, Miss Walker. Looks like a mass conspiracy. We'll hold you with the other two. Now, while we're at it, anyone else want to confess?"

Davis raged at him. "Don't be so damned funny. What am I supposed to do now. Why didn't they shoot me? I might as well be dead. We're ruined . . . finished! I suppose I'll have to pay all of you off tomorrow. And Equity will make me pay you for the next two weeks too, and rail fares in addition. And I'll have to pay those expensive jobbers who are coming up Monday."

His rage simmered down to a wail. Dr. Strong pointed at the covered corpse.

"There's one actor you won't have to pay . . . Sinclair Turner."

"Thanks. The only actor I ever got ahead of—a dead one."

The trooper impatiently kept looking at his wristwatch. No one had offered to move since his suggestion that some of them remove their makeup and get dressed. Ellen looked like she was going to be sick. He could understand how squeamish she'd be in the presence of the body. He decided to move them all downstairs so that if any of them wanted to go to the toilet or make any move anxiously to a dressing room, he'd be there to stop them or at least make a note of any suspicious movement. He gave his instructions to Dr. Strong.

"I'll go downstairs with all of them. And you, Doc, please stay here with the corpse. Don't let anyone touch anything and let me know the minute the chief gets here."

At that moment Bobby came rushing onstage from the stage

door. He quickly surveyed the scene and then started to jabber.

"My gawd! Why didn't someone tell me?"

Dobrow glared at him. "That's all we had on our minds."

"How about my pictures of the set? I've got the photographer outside in my car."

"I think the wrong man was shot." Dobrow was disgusted.

Bobby wailed at Davis, "V.D., you promised me pictures."

"Don't call me V.D.!" Davis was livid.

"You promised . . . "

"I was promised live actors, not dead ones."

19

Denouement

Halfway to stage right, as he led the group toward the steps to the dressing rooms, a thought occurred to Wally. He stopped and asked Dobrow, "Oh, Mr. Dobrow, where do you keep the blank cartridges for the gun?"

"In a box on the prop tables near the dimmer board."

"Let's get them."

The two crossed back to stage left, into the wings. The tables stood two feet back from the tormentor. Dobrow looked all over the table, then turned incredulously to the trooper.

"It's gone. I left the box right here."

Dobrow stooped down and started to look at the floor all around the table. His search yielded nothing.

"When did you last see it there."

"It was here at the last intermission. I checked it myself."

"Maybe you placed the box in your pocket, you know, sort of absentmindedly."

"A stage manager has no business being absentminded. Here, search me yourself."

"I will, just for the sake of form so that I can report that I did. Nothing personal."

Sam shrugged as he mumbled, "It's your job," and submitted to a personal search.

"Hand me your flashlight."

The trooper took the flashlight from Sam and started a methodical search in the area of stage left.

Onstage, Marc was suddenly struck with an idea. He hurried over to Davis who sat mournfully with his head in his hands.

"Listen to this, Vergil. I've got a wow of an idea."

"Oh noooo! I can't take any more of anything. I just want to lie down alongside poor Sinclair over there and let the world roll over me."

"Now listen to me. This isn't like you to be such a damned crybaby. Here's the poop: why can't we continue the way we planned it? You'll play Sinclair's role and I'll play Scotty, or the other way around? What do you say?"

"And who'll play Valerie?"

"She will. We'll talk to her."

"Provided you get the police to let her, provided she doesn't claim this made her sick and she can't go on, provided ... I can think of dozens of reasons why it's a screwy idea. Forget it. It's impossible. This scandal will ruin us. I know these yokels. Not only won't they come to this godforsaken theater, we'll be lucky if they don't run us out of town."

"I predict you're wrong."

"I predict we're through."

"Come on. Where's that old Vergil Davis slogan: the only thing predictable in the theater is that it's unpredictable."

"Try a little predicting exactly how we're going to live this down. Predict where I'm going to get the money to get my wife's jewelry out of the hock shop where I got the money for the Equity bond. Predict where I'm going to get the money to refund the advertisers for the rest of the season after we have to close down, money for refunds for the advance sales.... Some help you are with your corny philosophy and cockeyed ideas. You've got a lot at stake here, too. What chance will you have now of revealing yourself as the author? Go tell the world your play closed in the middle of opening night. God,

I've had plays close in a week. This one couldn't last even one night!"

"O.K. You win. You want me to fold my tent and silently crawl away—doomed to oblivion? I won't crawl anymore ... I won't ... "

"Face the damned facts of life and don't give me this whining, philosophical bullshit. You're supposed to be the creative mind in this team. Where's the old fire-eater? Think of something, for crissakes ... "

Getting no response from the other, suddenly Davis turned deathly quiet. He made certain no one could hear him, then he turned to Marc and whispered.

"My God, Marc ... you ... you didn't kill him, did you?"

"No, of course not. But if he were alive, I could kill him right now."

Was he being entirely honest with Vergil? Marc bethought himself about that live letter in his pocket. Was he not some kind of an accessory for not having gone with it to the police? And that record .... He reproached himself for not having done anything about the warnings even though he tried to squeeze some exoneration for his inaction out of the multifaceted rationale with which he tried to comfort himself. But now, what excuse could he have for failing to bring them to the attention of the police? After all, they may provide the clue to the killer. No matter what, his course was now clear. Resolutely, he turned to consult Vergil

"I think I have a clue to the identity of the killer."

With pistol-shot speed, Vergil turned to him, "Who?"

"I don't know precisely who he is. But he must be the one who sent me this letter." He handed the letter to Vergil with, "I had better turn this over to the police."

Vergil took it, perfunctorily looked at the envelope, and surprisingly didn't bother to open it. He spoke wearily.

"Oh, that. I know all about it. I sent it to you."

Marc gasped in shock, "Why? You don't realize what you did to me ... "

Davis impatiently brushed away his protestations. "So, all right. Now I realize how dumb the idea was. I forgot that you wouldn't react like a normal human being. Anyone else would have taken it to the police, or to the newspapers, or in some way raised a stink. I counted on your doing something, anything, and we'd get a trillion dollars worth of publicity out of it. Oh, but not you, you've got to be the Lone Ranger, the big silent hero . . . "

"And that Stanley Kowalski record . . . ?"

"Yeah, yeah," Vergil continued with the Marlon Brando dialect. "Dat wuz me all right. But ya didn't bite, so what da hell."

Marc glared at him incredulously. Vergil tried a placating grin. Seeing the trooper and Sam returning onto the stage, Marc walked away from Davis to brood by himself.

"Everyone will have to be searched . . . ," the trooper started to say when he was suddenly interrupted by an urgent cry from Marilyn.

"Joseph is sick. He's going to faint. Please help me, somebody . . . "

"Here, let me look at him," It was the doctor who rushed to her and grabbed the limp youth.

With Marilyn's assistance, the doctor helped Joseph to a chair. He started to take the groaning actor's pulse while he motioned to Marilyn.

"Hand me a glass and that decanter of water."

Joseph, as though stupefied, pushed the glass away. "I don't want any. I think I'm going to vomit."

The doctor felt his forehead and urged him to lean way forward.

"Now, son, I'm the doctor. Do as I tell you and you'll be all right in a jiffy."

Instead of succumbing to the doctor's gentle voice, Joseph turned fiercely on him.

"I don't want anything. I don't need a doctor. I just want to go to my dressing room and lie down."

At this point the trooper took over.

"You can lie down on this couch."

The occupants of the sofa moved away. The trooper took Joseph's hand to lead him to the sofa. Joseph snatched away his hand and screamed hysterically.

"I don't want to stay here. I can't stand this place. I've got to get out of here . . ."

He started to weave about the stage when the doctor intercepted him.

"How about a shot of brandy, Joseph? I've got some in my bag."

Not waiting for a reply, the doctor quickly went off to stage left and returned with his black bag. From it he took out a small flask and offered Joseph a drink.

"No. I don't want anything. I just want to get out of here."

"You need a sedative."

Joseph eagerly turned to him, "Do you have some sort of pill?"

"Let me see," the doctor said as he looked into his bag. "No, but I can inject it."

"Never mind. Don't bother. Maybe I will take some brandy."

"No bother, Joseph. Roll up your sleeve."

The doctor turned away from Joseph and took out a hypodermic needle which he started to prepare for the injection. He did not see Joseph backing away from him. When he turned in readiness for the injection, Joseph had edged half way across the stage. The doctor determinedly approached him.

"No!"

Joseph's cry was a desperate wail. Dr. Strong nodded to the trooper, who quickly rushed Joseph and held him in an unbreakable grip. The panic-stricken youth struggled as though he was in fear of the most frightful torture. The trooper soon had him subdued and held him despite his writhing.

"Let me go," he gasped. "You can't do this . . ."

Denouement

"Hold him, now, Wally. I'm just going to roll up his sleeve."

Despite Joseph's kicking and screaming, the doctor succeeded in rolling up his sleeve. After a quick look at the exposed arm, the doctor walked back to his bag and replaced the needle without having made the injection.

"All right, Wally, you can let him go. No, Joseph. I'm not giving you any injection. You've had too many."

The doctor spoke to the trooper.

"Did you see those marks, Wally? Looks like a battlefield. There's the answer to who pilfered my medicine bag."

He then turned to Joseph, "You stole a hypodermic and a large quantity of drugs from my bag."

The look of shock on Joseph's face looked genuine enough, and his words had the semblance of truth, "I don't know what you're talking about. I never touched your bag. I never saw it before this minute."

"Where'd you get it then?"

"Sinclair gave it to me. The needle is in his room."

The trooper now accused him. "You certainly know that, son. You put it there yourself."

"I did not. I'm not a thief. I never stole anything in my life. I . . ."

"Take it easy, son," the doctor said as he cautioned the trooper to desist. "I believe you. We'll find the needle, I'm sure. But, how about the drug? How did you get hold of it?"

"From Sinclair."

"That's too easy, son," the trooper could not restrain himself from interrupting the doctor's interrogation of Joseph. "Sinclair, of course, can't very well deny it, can he?"

"I never knew where he hid it. I admit I looked for it."

"I looked for it, too. It's not in Mr. Turner's room," the doctor said significantly to the trooper.

"I think I will take some brandy, with water, please," Joseph weakly pleaded with the doctor.

"You can take a slug out of the flask directly," said the

doctor as he handed the flask to him.

Joseph gulped the brandy from the flask while the doctor filled a glass with some water from the decanter and handed the glass to Joseph who awkwardly handed back the flask. In the exchange, the glass somehow slipped out of Joseph's hand and fell to the floor and spilled completely out.

As the doctor reached down to retrieve the glass, he calmly said to Joseph, "That won't help, Joseph. There's more of the evidence in the decanter."

Joseph made a dash for the decanter, but he was too late, for the trooper had grabbed the decanter out of Joseph's reach. Quickly, the trooper handed the decanter to the doctor while he made certain to hold on to Joseph.

The others had watched the brief drama with Joseph in amazement. The doctor turned to Valerie and Ellen.

"Ladies, your playacting was superb. Worthy of Duse. But it was all unnecessary. Wally, I'm sure you can tell the others they're free to go as they please."

"That's right," said the trooper as he prepared to lead Joseph to the door.

Dobrow stood in his way. "Do you mean to say that Junior here substituted the bullet?"

"I think Dr. Strong can best explain it to you," replied the trooper.

They all turned to the doctor. "When I pronounced Sinclair Turner dead, I did not say how he died. He did not die of a bullet wound, simply because he was not shot. The shot was a blank all right, as they all were. And Wally, the missing blanks are under that canvass in the dead man's pocket. Don't ask me why. As for the cause of death . . . Sinclair Turner died of an overdose of a drug. During his last scene he drank copiously from that decanter, which I presume Joseph filled . . ."

"That's right," Dobrow interjected excitedly in verifying the doctor's statement. "I asked Joseph to do me a favor and fill the jug."

"There you have it," continued the doctor. "There was enough of the drug there to kill an elephant. His staggering was no pretense; it was all too real. Meanwhile, he was terrified, petrified by the mounting horror in his mind—of reliving that actual moment of years ago when the gun was pointed at him for real." Dr. Strong looked significantly at Marilyn and then continued. "You might say he was frightened to death. The psychological shock accelerated the deadly impact of the fatal drug. An interesting coincidence, we might say, of psychology and physiology."

He paused, and all reflected momentarily on his words.

As the trooper led Joseph out, Davis screamed at him, "You, you son-of-an-actor, you . . ."

20

Mummers and Men

The peaceful, slow-moving Merrimac was oblivious to the passions of the mummers the next morning as it quietly flowed to the sea. Quite early, Everett and Valerie met by its banks, and after an embrace they walked along its path hand in hand. They had made no plans to meet, yet by some unspoken intuition in a language known only to lovers, each knew he would find his love once again at that precise moment at that precise spot by the stream.

Untypically for actors, neither one had stopped to read the morning papers to learn once again of a real-life drama in which each had played a principal role. Had they done so, they would have learned that the audience, although free to leave after the arrest of young Joseph, lingered about the theater as though reluctant to leave the scene of a great drama that had been enacted before their eyes. For years to come they would be telling newcomers to the area about that exciting night.

Endicott's weekly newspaper came out with a special edition in the hope it may have scooped the nation. Alas, the network of newspapers had its ways with the police, and the bizarre story was featured on the front pages of the newspapers across the nation. The New York papers had a special story via wire report of how Joseph J. Heyward received the news of his son's arrest just as he was about to sit down to a dinner party for celebrities in honor of his son's debut in the theater.

    Backstage at the theater, Dobrow ruefully contemplated the set and then went about straightening out the furniture and clearing away items left over from the night before. In row D of the auditorium, in the center, Marilyn was adjusting photographic equipment that was set up on a tripod. Her uninterrupted chatter did not seem to disturb the stage manager. Actually, it elicited an occasional smile and an indulgent comment.

    "My father wasn't too bad on the phone. But my mother! Gosh! She still doesn't believe that I wasn't the one that was shot. They got the first version of the shooting, didn't stop to hear the rest of the broadcast, and immediately started to phone me. All the phone lines for fifty miles around, I bet, were all tied up, and they didn't get me till three o'clock in the morning. Then I told them about the poisoning. That's when she begged me to drink bottled soda only. She should know I've been living on cokes. And my father, all he kept asking was if I had gone out on any dates with Sinclair Turner or with Joseph. Finally, I got angry and told them, all right! I said, 'You're not worried if maybe one of them broke my heart. All you're worried about is my status as a virgin.' I think that settled it. I had to open my big mouth. He'll settle for a Wasserman."

    "Parents and theater don't mix."

    "They got me real sore. I lost my cool and said I was going to elope with Bobby Francis so I could go to my grave as pure and virginal as the day I was born. I think my father fainted at that point. Well, they'll be up tonight or tomorrow to take me home. I'll sweat out the summer at their bourgeois swim club catching up on my math. I'd almost settle for that cruddy camp I used to go to with all those drippy kids."

    An excited Bobby came running down the aisle.

    "Are we all ready?"

    For an answer he got a growl from Dobrow, "Yes, we're all ready. You might have been here on time yourself. I got no sleep all night and I get here early—so where's Mr. Bobby Francis? Nowhere in sight. I must have been crazy to promise you . . ."

"Now don't spoil it all with a bad temper. You've no idea how much I appreciate this. Full lights now on the entire set."

Dobrow went beyond the tormentors on stage left and operated the control board. He brought up all the lights. Bobby cautioned Marilyn to be ready while he focused the camera with considerable expertise. He called out to Dobrow.

"Please raise the scrim. I want to get the room alone."

Sam obliged. Bobby made certain that Marilyn was on the ready with a special flashbulb in addition to the one on the camera, but connected to the same push button. He signaled her to raise the device, and then he shot the picture. He then moved Marilyn to the right and took another shot. Then he gave his instructions again.

"Please lower the scrim and kill all lights except those in front of it."

Again the stage manager obliged, and Bobby took a few more pictures. Finally, he asked for all lights on to capacity with the scrim still down. The effect he sought was to show the set within a set. Marilyn moved on instructions from Bobby from one side to the other as he took three more pictures. Then he called out to Dobrow that he was through and that Dobrow could kill the lights. Just then Ellen came in through the stage door, down through the center of the set.

"I'm not too late, am I?"

"You may be a slave to time, but we don't let it encroach upon our conscience. We live oblivious of the moment . . ." Marilyn's flippancy was interrupted by all lights instantaneously bursting on to their full power and Sam eagerly running on to the stage.

"No, you're never late. Hold the camera, Bobby. Don't pack it up. Take a few shots of Ellen and me."

During Bobby's preoccupation with setting up the camera again, with Marilyn's assistance, Sam questioned Ellen.

"I phoned my agent in New York. He wasn't in yet, but his girl said she thinks he can get me two weeks as a jobber in Pennsylvania. How about you?"

"I don't know. I haven't had time to think."

"I've had time. I've been thinking of you and how wonderfully brave you were last night. And your defending me . . . But, I'm puzzled about you and Sinclair. How come he offered to marry you? Did you lead him on? When did all this happen? We were here only a little over a week and we were all so goddamned busy . . ."

"Now don't start with me, Sam. I'm letting you know right now, from the very beginning, that I'm not going to go through life with a jealous husband."

"Wha . . . what did you say? But . . . I . . . oh my God . . . Darling!"

Of course their long kiss and spontaneous embrace was lingering.

"Hold it!" The flashlight bulbs exploded as Bobby took their picture. They were oblivious to everyone but themselves.

"Hey, the picture is over. Hey, you two . . ." They ignored Marilyn's yelling.

Not until Everett's entrance in a few moments did they detach themselves from each other. He was uncommonly cheerful—for Everett.

"Good morning, everybody. Hey, why aren't all of you packing?"

"Testimonials, credits, pictures, and so on," Marilyn volunteered. "Are you ready for yours?"

"Why not? We'll compare them with the rogues' gallery shots the newspapers took last night."

Bobby wailed, "Yes, I saw a couple of them in the Boston papers this morning. Such clutter, clutter, clutter! It didn't look like my sets at all."

A very harassed-looking Vergil Davis, unshaven, still in his tuxedo, in which he probably slept briefly, dragged himself down the aisle from the front of the house. With a weak smile he diffidently acknowledged their greetings. He called for silence.

"O.K., everybody. I want your attention. I'll get word to the others at their boarding houses. I've arranged transportation for all of you back to New York. If anyone decides he wants to stay on for a few days, let me know by two o'clock. Everyone else be ready by nine tomorrow morning. The usual notice will be up in an hour. It's being typed now. It will answer all questions. You will all get your week's pay tonight before dinner. Next week's check will be distributed within two weeks by mail from my office or from Equity."

An awkward pause was the only response.

"Well, I guess that's it. You're a good bunch and deserve a better break . . ."

Ellen quickly interrupted him.

"Don't look so glum. Take a picture with us."

In the midst of a chorus of pleading and encouragement for Davis to join them in a group picture, Marc came on stage.

"May I join the wake?"

With a glowering bravado, Davis joined the others for the group picture.

"Irresponsible and improvident, the lot of you. That's all you can think of . . . pictures! What in hell am I doing here? I should have cut my throat and laid myself down alongside poor Sinclair."

Bobby and Marilyn snickered, while Ellen tried to cheer him.

"You know you can't live without us."

"I won't know till I try it. I'll have plenty opportunities from now on, I'm sure."

"How should we take the picture, Marc?" It was Bobby who busied himself with the camera.

"Let's make it a tableau curtain call—the one we missed last night."

The others started to make suggestions when Davis offered the decision.

"Good idea, Marc. Places . . ."

"Please," Everett stopped them by holding up his hand. "Let's wait till Valerie gets here. It'll only be a couple of minutes."

"Good idea," Davis replied. "Meanwhile, we don't need all those lights. Sam, kill them till we're ready. And Ellen, please go up front and watch the store. If anyone comes to the box office for refunds, tell them to mail in the tickets and we'll mail them a check. There's been a mob up front for hours. I've been afraid to open the box office. I just can't figure out their morbid curiosity. They just stand around. I never saw such a traffic jam. It was all I could do to run through that gauntlet."

"All right, Mr. Davis. But don't be long. I've got to pack."

"O.K., O.K. The regular box-office help should be there any minute to relieve you."

Sam encouraged her, "I'll help you pack later. They may need an ingenue or leading lady in Pennsylvania. I need one, that's sure."

"You've got one." With that, Ellen quickly kissed him and hurried up the aisle.

With businesslike pragmatism, Davis started to give orders.

"Sam, you'll take Marilyn and Bobby, and anyone else you can get to help, and get all lighting equipment up here and ready for shipment. After lunch, we'll strike the set. You can start now. We'll call you the moment Valerie gets here for the pictures."

The three members of the crew left Davis and Marc to themselves.

The two men simply stared at each other silently.

The producer was the first to break the silence.

"Spare me any Pollyannish banalities. I've been on the spot before and managed to survive."

He paused and then laughed. "This will probably go down in the annals of the theater as the most publicized flop in history. A closing that hit the front pages from coast to coast."

"I'm sorry," Marc answered him.

"Don't be sorry for me. Be sorry for yourself, chum."

Valerie came in fron the stage door.

"What a horde around the theater! Cars are just piling up by the minute. A man told me there's a traffic jam on the turnpike halfway to Boston."

Hearing her voice, Everett came on stage from the wings on the right.

Marc and Davis greeted her. With a knowing signal to Marc, Davis said, "I don't care if the mob tears down the place. Come on, Marc, let's go see how the kids are getting on. Oh yes, Valerie, we've been waiting for you to take a group picture. We'll be here in a few minutes, so you two please hang around."

The two men went out, down the stairs.

"Feel any better?" Valerie asked Everett.

"Still numb."

"We've been through a lot."

He moodily nodded to her and walked around the stage. She continued.

"You didn't answer me this morning. Are you going back to New York?"

"I may stay a few days. How about you?"

"No plans. I may stay a while, unless these mobs scare me away."

It was quite obvious to her that he wanted to talk, but he didn't. She decided to help him.

"I enjoyed our walk along the river . . . I'd like us to do it again."

"Oh, Valerie . . .," He moved toward her.

"Oh, my darling. It's been so terribly long."

They were eager for each other, yet tender and understanding. She gently untwined herself.

"Oh, Scotty, it's not going to be the happy ending so easily."

"It was a happy ending for me last night when you said it

was you who had substituted the bullet."

"I came in on cue. It was a line from a play I must have seen or was in so many centuries ago. But Scotty, a revelation, an act of faith and love doesn't root out the cause of doubt, all the bitterness that has made you feel so miserable. Will you, please ..."

"Maybe, my darling. I may give it a try. We'll see when we get back to New ... back home. But I know you're going to be my best therapy."

"How romantic—a therapeutic marriage ..."

His kisses muffled the rest of what she would say. They turned to the sound of a loud, artificial cough. Dr. Strong stood to their left with a proud grin all over his face.

"Don't say anything, my friends. I just want to shake your hands, bless you, and wish you luck."

During the handshakes, Everett effusively thanked the doctor. Then the doctor looked around in puzzlement.

"Where's everybody?"

"Packing up things. Getting ready to silently steal away."

"They don't really have to. I spoke to the chief selectman this morning. He had been on the phone with the other selectmen, and they all agreed to play along with Mr. Davis and the company if Mr. Davis agrees to stay."

Everett exchanged looks with Valerie, then he replied.

"That would be up to Mr. Davis. We'd love to stay. But I think Davis believes he's been jinxed here. His plans are pretty well set now. We're all to be paid off by tonight."

"That's a pity. This area is starved for good, live theater. I had hopes we'd tear the people away from their television sets and give them an idea of what they're missing. And there are lots of people around here, and probably all over the country, who believe the same way I do."

"Davis is many things," Valerie said, "but a missionary he is not. Oh, I don't mean he isn't a decent sort as producers go. But he's got to survive, you know."

"I don't want to change the subject, but how about that

poor kid, Joseph?" asked Everett.

"He confessed to the whole business. He said he really didn't mean to kill Sinclair Turner. He just wanted to throw a scare into him, knock him out for a while. It seems he also got some drugs from a couple who had been caught with him a couple of nights ago. They're now in hot water, conspiracy to do bodily harm and so on. They won't get off easily. As for Joseph, I've committed him to Mass. General Hospital until he is tried. His father and mother are flying in from the coast."

They heard a frantic cry from up the front of the house. Ellen beseeched them.

"Please, where's Mr. Davis?"

Everett yelled back to her, "He's down in the dressing rooms."

"Please get him in a hurry. I need help. I can't hold back the mob. Tell him to get the police . . . please hurry . . ."

She dashed back out the front door.

Everett ran to the stair and called down to Davis; then he went back to Valerie and the doctor.

"Maybe I should go up front to help her . . ."

The doctor cautioned him, "You stay put right here. That's just what the mob wants, to see the man who held the gun."

A testy Davis came up the stair; he was followed by Marc. They exchanged greetings with the doctor.

"What's wrong now, Scotty? What's bothering you?"

"It's Ellen. She's being mobbed. She said maybe you should get the police."

Davis turned to Marc. "Please, Marc. I can't face them. You go. If you have any problems, call the police. The number is right alongside the phone."

Marc jumped off the stage and strode quickly up the aisle. Then Davis turned to the actors.

"We'll get to that picture-taking yet. Meanwhile you two better get your stuff out of the dressing rooms."

He paused, and then continued with a wan smile, "Hope

you have a longer run next time."
 Valerie tried to say something, "I can't tell you how sorry we are, Mr. Davis ..."
 "That's all right, kids. I always said there's a crisis every hour in summer stock. This one is a lulu—a crisis to end all crises. The next one I'll have to face is that hungry mob up front. They're after my scalp. Refunds ... and I've no money. Money—my God, I'll have to settle up some way with the people in New York who advanced me the loot for this summer."
 "What'll you do?" asked Everett.
 "That's an interesting question ..."
 "I think I can help you with ...," started the doctor.
 Davis gratefully waved him down. "You've been wonderful, doctor. They don't come any better than you. But money won't open this theater. The black eye ..."
 "The selectmen don't agree. They have faith in you. And after all, this tragedy wasn't your fault. You can't be blamed the least bit. The chief selectman told me for himself and for the town that you can continue here for the rest of the summer. They might even help out by cutting down on the rent."
 The producer looked at the doctor and did not immediately reply. Then he slowly said, "My instincts about this place were right. This has been a costly disappointment to me, but by God, I never met a more wonderful bunch of people ..."
 "Don't be hasty in making a decision. Think it over. What other plans do you have?"
 "Hmmn. I'll go back to New York and revive a classic, maybe. Or maybe I'll actually read one of the new plays the agents have been sending me. Of course I can always cut my throat. Then again, I can get out of the theater and get a job in some calm, sane industry. No, I think I had better cut my throat."
 Marc suddenly burst through the front door and came charging down the aisle.
 "Vergil—Vergil—"

He jumped up on stage and stood there breathlessly grinning at Davis.

"So, out with it."

"You'll never believe this . . ."

"If you don't talk I'll strangle you, you son of a bitch . . ."

"Hold everything! Now be calm. Maybe you better sit down . . ."

"Talk already, you . . ." Davis screamed at him.

"That mob up front . . . There are thousands of people up there, all of them waving money. They want to buy tickets . . . you can sell out for the next fifty years. We can run this show forever!"

Marc turned to Valerie and Everett and hugged them. A changed Davis, a jubilant Davis started to scream incoherently. He shook the doctor's hands, both of them, he hugged the others. Apparently attracted by the tumult, Dobrow, Marilyn, and Bobby came running up onto the stage. Valerie and Everett explained the excitement to them. Davis stood up on a chair and addressed the others.

"This calls for a celebration. Sam, bring up that champagne we have down in your dressing room. Marc, you're the director. Either you play Sinclair's role or I'll play it myself. And I'll check that gun myself, personally before the third act every night . . ."

"You're on, Vergil," Marc gleefully shouted back to him. "I cast myself in the role . . ."

"I've got a better idea," said Everett. "Why not let Dr. Strong play the role and either one of you or Sam can play the judge."

They all turned toward the doctor.

"I think I can handle it. I once played the villainous Richard III."

"Then we're all set," said the businesslike Marc. "We start a run-through of the Sinclair scenes right after lunch so we'll be ready tonight. And Vergil, get your announcements out that we're running this play an extra week. With all this excitement we won't be able to get into rehearsal for the next bill on Monday."

"You've got a deal. we're all set then."

They were all startled again by Ellen's shouts as she came running down the aisle.

"Mr. Davis ... Mr. Davis ... Look what just arrived. Read these telegrams ..."

She reached the foot of the apron and thrust a batch of telegrams at Davis who had come downstage to meet her. He fumbled through the telegrams while the others, fearful of what they may contain, silently huddled as far from him as they could manage. They were electrified by a sudden, hoarse cry from him. The doctor rushed toward him as he saw him staggering and clutching at his collar. Davis brushed the doctor aside and started to let out a series of war whoops. He suddenly stopped, then quietly looked all around at the others. A grin started and then spread all over his face, and he again started to laugh.

"I don't believe it."

He handed the telegram he had opened to Marc.

"Here, Marc, you read it. I want to see if what I read is true ..."

A puzzled Marc took the telegram, glanced through it, let out a yell and embraced Davis.

"That's not fair ..."

"Let us in on it ..."

The others crowded around the dancing two. Marc sobered and started to read:

"Offer 100,000 with escalation clause pending Broadway production. Signed, Warner Brothers."

All of them started to cheer.

Marilyn was the first to comment, "They managed to get it said just under ten words."

Amidst all the jubilation and congratulations, Davis called for Sam.

"I'm hoarse. Where's Sam with that champagne?"

"Here's another," shouted Marc. He read another telegram, "Will top any offer. Arriving tonight. Signed, Wilson, 20th Century Films."

"Any more of them?" Davis was quite hoarse.

Marc continued to read, "Listen to this, 'Offer you any of our theaters for your show, Signed, Shubert Theaters.' And here's a cable from London ..."

"Here, let me have them."

Davis took the batch from Marc, and started to read them. He walked toward the table with the decanter and glass and poured himself some water. Then he started to read again. Suddenly he stopped, gasped, and staggered. In consternation the others became transfixed. He pointed in terror toward the decanter.

"That's it ... I drank the poisoned water ... my God ... Dr. Strong ... quick ... help me ... get me to a hospital."

While Everett and Marc rushed to support him and half carry him out with the doctor leading the way, Sam whispered to Ellen, "V.D. is the biggest ham actor of them all."